IT'S BEGINNING TO LOOK A LOT LIKE CHRISTMAS . . .

"So this is the errand Carole mentioned her dad had to run," Stevie said. "I smell a rat, don't you?"

"Sure, but it's a Christmas rat," Lisa reminded her. "They are white and they tell white lies."

"We're shopping for Carole. How about you?" Stevie asked when Colonel Hanson came up to them.

"Me too," he said. "I have something in mind for her big present, but I want some little things to put in her stocking and under the tree."

"Her big present is so big it doesn't fit under the tree?" Lisa asked, impressed.

"Nope," the colonel said. "And that reminds me that I've been meaning to call you girls. I can use your help. Why don't we step over to Pizza Man across the way there and have a little talk?"

"I'm never too full of junk food to say no to pizza," Stevie said, leading the way.

In a few minutes, Colonel Hanson and the girls were settled into a booth, a pepperoni, sausage, and mushroom pizza cooking especially for them.

"So, how can we help?" Stevie asked, getting down to business. . . .

THE SADDLE CLUB

STARLIGHT CHRISTMAS

BONNIE BRYANT

A BANTAM SKYLARK BOOK®
NEW YORK • TORONTO • LONDON • SYDNEY • AUCKLAND

I would like to express my special thanks
and appreciation to Bruce H. Koenig,
D.V.M., and to Arline Harms.

RL 5, 009–012

STARLIGHT CHRISTMAS
A Bantam Skylark Book / November 1990

ISBN 0-553-15832-5

Published simultaneously in the United States and Canada

PRINTED IN THE UNITED STATES OF AMERICA

OPM   0 9 8 7 6 5 4 3 2 1

For Emmons and Andy

1

THE SCHOOL HALLS echoed with cheerful wishes for a merry Christmas and happy holidays. Lockers banged shut, not to be opened again for two and a half weeks, when school resumed after the new year. Three students skipped down the hallway, holding hands and singing loudly, "Hark the herald angels sho-out! Now's the day that we get out!"

Carole Hanson was oblivious to all the cheer. She felt distant from the activity around her. Christmases had been hard for her and her father since her mother's death almost two years earlier. Most of the time, Carole could accept that her mother was gone. But it was difficult to do that at Christmas. More than anything, Carole wanted this Christmas to be better. Merry was too much to ask for.

She thought about her father. She had been working on his main present for over a month. She was knitting him a pair of argyle socks. Colonel Hanson was crazy about certain things, and that included argyle socks. Carole knew he'd love the set she was making for him. If she could make him happy, then her Christmas would be a good one.

"See you next year, Carole!" one of her classmates said, and giggled at the weak joke. Carole smiled thinly. She closed her own locker and turned to leave school for vacation.

The vacation loomed ahead of her as a long, empty period. The only good thing about it was that she would have more time to spend with the horses at Pine Hollow Stables, where she rode. Horses were everything to Carole. When she grew up, she planned to work with them. She wasn't sure if she would raise them, train them, heal them, or ride them. Maybe she'd do all of those things.

Carole tucked a few loose strands of her curly black hair into her wool hat. She was just reaching for the door when a familiar voice stopped her.

"Wait up, Carole!" Lisa Atwood called, hurrying down the hallway.

"Can you believe it?" she asked when she had caught up with her friend. "Two weeks without school. Nothing but Christmas and horses!" She smiled excitedly, and Carole couldn't help smiling as well. Lisa put her arm across Carole's shoulders and gave her a squeeze. Carole was glad Lisa was there.

Lisa Atwood was one of Carole's two best friends, but she was very different from Carole. She was a year older, although she didn't seem it. She was an excellent student, and she usually got straight A's. Like Carole, Lisa loved horses and riding, but her lessons had to be squeezed in between ballet and piano and whatever else Mrs. Atwood thought was an appropriate kind of lesson for a proper young lady. Lisa didn't mind doing the other things as long as it meant that she could ride. She'd do anything to ride!

Their other best friend was Stevie—short for Stephanie—Lake. Stevie was as horse crazy as her two best friends, and she also rode at Pine Hollow, but that was where their similarities ended. Stevie was as mischievous around horses as Carole was dedicated, as easygoing a student as Lisa was serious. Her strongest point was fun. Whenever something wasn't going the way the girls wanted it to, Stevie could always think up some kind of wild scheme that would make it right. Her schemes usually worked, too, though sometimes not the way the girls expected!

It didn't matter to any of the three of them that they were different from one another. They were friends because of what they had in common: They were horse crazy. In fact, they were so horse crazy that they'd started

The Saddle Club. It only had two rules: Members had to be horse crazy, and they had to be willing to help one another, no matter what. Sometimes that meant sharing riding tips. Sometimes it meant working together on things like science projects. But it always meant fun.

"Did Stevie call you last night?" Lisa asked.

Carole shook her head.

"We've got a ride to the mall this afternoon. We're going Christmas shopping. Want to come?"

"I can't," Carole said regretfully. "My main gift is Dad's socks, and I've still got one whole foot to go. He's got some errand he has to run today, so I'll have time at home to work on it."

"Oh." Lisa looked disappointed. "Well, we're meeting at TD's. Do you have time for a Saddle Club meeting?"

"I *always* have time for a Saddle Club meeting," Carole said. She would have liked to have been with her friends at the mall, but the trip to TD's was the next best thing. Tastee Delight was a local ice cream place and the girls' favorite—and most fattening—hangout. It was within walking distance of Stevie's and Lisa's houses, and of Pine Hollow. It was also near the bus stop Carole used to get home. The girls called it TD's for short and often had their Saddle Club meetings there.

Together, Lisa and Carole walked to the shopping center where TD's was located. A few stray snowflakes drifted down out of the sky. Lisa saw them as a sign that

Christmas was coming. Carole didn't seem to see them at all.

Stevie was already ensconced in a booth at TD's when the girls joined her. "Christmas vacation," she said as they sat down. She sounded as if she were savoring the words. "No school, lots of free time, lots of *riding* time, no school, and then . . ." She paused for effect. "New Year's Eve."

"What's so special about that?" Lisa asked, teasing her friend. She and Carole both knew that Stevie was beyond teasing when it came to this New Year's Eve.

"Did you forget?" Stevie asked. "It's the big dance. I'm going with Phil. I can't wait."

"I was joking," Lisa informed her drily. "So what's the highlight of your vacation going to be, Carole?"

Carole pursed her lips. If Christmas wasn't going to be all that great for her, it was hard to think what was going to be. Then she remembered. "Easy," she said. "Christmas Eve—the Starlight Ride."

"Oh, right!" Stevie agreed. "I almost forgot. So my vacation will have *two* highlights—not counting no school, which would make it three."

"This will be my first time, you know," Lisa reminded her friends.

"You're going to love the starlight ride," Carole promised. "It's just wonderful. I think it's one of my favorite Pine Hollow traditions."

"Tell me about it," Lisa said.

Carole was about to begin when their waitress arrived. As soon as the waitress spotted Stevie, she grimaced. Stevie was famous for ordering outrageous sundaes. She'd even been accused of ordering them that way so nobody would be tempted to take little tastes from her dish. Stevie always flatly denied it, and continued to order new and generally unappetizing combinations of flavors. The waitress never liked to take orders when Stevie was around. This time, as usual, Carole and Lisa each ordered normal sundaes. The waitress turned to Stevie, expectantly braced for the worst.

"I'll just have a diet cola," Stevie said.

The waitress looked astonished. "That's it? No bubble-gum ice-cream float? No marshmallow sauce on top?"

Stevie made a face. "Ugh," she said. "No way. Just a soda, please."

Relieved, the waitress left.

"Why didn't you get ice cream?" Lisa asked.

"Well, I have to fit into my dress for the New Year's Eve dance, don't I?"

Lisa and Carole looked at their slender friend in surprise.

"So what are you wearing that you're having trouble fitting into?" Carole asked.

"I don't know," Stevie said. "I haven't bought it yet, but I want to be sure it fits when I do."

Lisa and Carole couldn't help 'themselves. They started laughing. Stevie laughed, too.

"So, back to the Starlight Ride," Lisa said. "Tell me about it."

"Right," Carole said. Carole and Stevie had been riding at Pine Hollow for a long time, while Lisa had only started six months earlier. She was an apt pupil and had learned a lot in that short period, but there were still certain traditions she didn't know about. Pine Hollow was owned and run by Max Regnery—the third-generation Regnery to do so. Max's mother, Mrs. Reg, was his business manager and a friend to all the kids who rode there. Since the stable had been in the Regnery family for so long, many Pine Hollow traditions had developed over the years. The Starlight Ride was one of everybody's favorites.

"On Christmas Eve, at about seven o'clock, all the young riders at Pine Hollow come to the stable and saddle up. We leave about seven-thirty. We follow a trail marked with lanterns that Max and the stablehands have laid out in the fields and through the woods. The trail leader carries a huge torch. Sometimes we sing Christmas carols and Hanukkah songs as we go. Anyway, we end up at the town center where there's a crèche and a menorah and we have a party."

"It sounds like a lot of fun," Lisa said.

"It's more than that," Stevie said. "It's magic. It's hard

to explain, though. It's just really wonderful. But Carole left out one of the most important things about it. Since she was the one who got the best-overall-rider award last summer, she's the one who will lead us all and carry the torch!"

"Wow!" Lisa said. "That's great! You won't get us lost, though, will you?"

"I think I can follow a path laid out by bright lanterns," Carole said. "And I'm sure that Barq won't let anything bad happen to me in between lanterns."

"How's that?" Lisa asked.

"Didn't you know that horses can see in the dark?" Stevie asked.

"No, I didn't know that," Lisa said. "But I do now. So how come we don't do a lot more riding at night?"

"Well, for the horses, it wouldn't be a problem. The problem is the people," Carole explained. "See, the horse doesn't know that his rider can't see, so he'll go wherever the rider tells him, even when his own eyes tell him better. He'll duck right under a low-slung branch that'll knock the rider right off his back."

Lisa didn't like the sound of that. "Could that happen on the Starlight Ride?"

"Oh, no," Carole assured her. "That's why Max lays out the trail first with the lanterns. We'll be fine. And it will be wonderful!"

"One dish of banana yogurt, one fudge sundae, and one diet cola," the waitress announced, putting the orders in front of them. Then she turned to Stevie. "Oh, and when I told the counterman what you'd ordered, he wanted me to check to see if you have a fever. I told him it wouldn't do any good. It's the other times you might be sick. For once, you're normal!"

Stevie nodded. Then, as the woman went away, she turned to her friends. "Whatever was that poor lady talking about?" she asked, tamping her straw down on the table to remove the wrapper. "Must be a very stressful job here, I guess."

The girls chatted as they finished their orders, alternating from horse talk to discussions of what kind of dress Stevie should get for the New Year's Eve dance. Soon, they were ready to leave and paid their bill. Mrs. Durham, the mother of one of their friends who rode at Pine Hollow, had offered to take Stevie and Lisa to the mall. The girls saw her car pull up to the curb. Mrs. Durham honked and Lisa and Stevie ran, leaving Carole to collect their change and leave a tip while she waited for her bus. She saw them wave gaily from the rear seat of the Durhams' station wagon as they left. Carole waved back.

She knew they'd have fun at the mall and she didn't mind. She wasn't really in a Christmas mood anyway. Being by herself, working on the sock, was a better idea for her for that afternoon.

The waitress brought their change. Carole figured out the tip, left it on the table, and stepped out into the cool December afternoon. She noticed the snowflakes this time as they drifted down through the streams of light from the parking-lot lamps. The flakes, so pretty and so delicate in the air, melted as they reached the ground, merging with all the other dampness that penetrated Carole's shoes. She quickly became cold and uncomfortable.

Carole's bus turned into the parking lot and honked. She waved and climbed aboard when it stopped. She paid her fare and took a seat. Soon she'd be home, working on making this Christmas better—the best ever. She was sure she could do it.

Yes, she told herself, *this Christmas will be good. Maybe.*

2

THE MALL, ALWAYS a fun place to be, was even more inviting in the holiday season. It seemed to Stevie and Lisa that every single store was bursting with beautiful, tempting things.

"Did you see those earrings?" Stevie asked, nudging Lisa. "Do you think Carole would like them?"

Lisa looked where Stevie pointed. The earrings in question were made of feathers and designed to dangle to the wearer's shoulders. The feathers were electric orange, with peacock-blue tips. Carole was a casual but conservative dresser. She usually wore little gold hoops or pearl-dot earrings. "I don't think those are really right for Carole," Lisa said as tactfully as she could. Then she saw the look on Stevie's face and continued, "But I really think the look is *you*, so I'll probably sneak back here and buy them for you later. Is that what you want?"

"For New Year's Eve," Stevie agreed. The girls giggled together.

They wandered through a lot of shops and department stores. What they both wanted, more than anything, was to get Carole something that would make her Christmas better.

"It's so hard, you know," Stevie said, sifting through a box of scarves that were on sale. "I mean, I know Carole will like whatever we give her, but we don't want to give her something that's just *nice;* we want to give her something that's perfect."

The girls abandoned scarves and wended their way to another counter.

"Fuzzy slippers?" Lisa said. Stevie shook her head. Lisa knew she was right. Carole wasn't the fuzzy slipper type.

"How about some funky socks?" Stevie suggested. It was worth a try. But all the socks seemed either too funky or not funky enough.

"Do you think she'd like a belt?" Stevie asked. They tried, but they had no better luck there.

It seemed that everywhere they turned in the mall, there were wonderful stores with marvelous things in the windows and on the racks and shelves, but there was nothing that was just right for Carole—nothing that could change another Christmas without her mother from okay to wonderful.

Stevie found a bright red nightshirt for her twin brother, Alex, and a book about horror movies for her older brother, Chad. Lisa found an elegant kitchen clock for her parents and a sweater for her brother.

"Maybe a book about horses?" Stevie offered. They spent a long time in the book department, but that only served to underline the basic problem: The only perfect present for Carole was a horse!

CAROLE LET HERSELF into the house and locked the door behind her. She had gotten used to coming home to an empty house, but that didn't make her like it. She turned on the lights, hung up her coat, and headed for her room. The unfinished socks were in a bag tucked under her bed. She took off her shoes, turned on her radio, and began to work on the foot. It wasn't hard. The tricky pattern work was finished. This section needed to be shaped, but the instructions were easy to follow. Besides, she'd already done the other foot. This was exactly the same.

Carole's coal-black kitten, Snowball, lay in a little ball at the foot of her bed. Carole had given her pet the name because it was as contrary as he was. It seemed that no matter what Carole told him to do, he did the exact opposite. Now, she wished he would wake up and keep her company. He usually wanted to play with the yarn as she knit anyway. But he was having none of it. He slept.

"Go to sleep, Snowball," she said. "Whatever you do,

don't come play with this yarn. And for goodness' sake, stay at the foot of the bed."

He did.

Carole was immediately suspicious. Snowball was nothing if not predictable. She'd never known him to do what she said. She put down her knitting and reached down to pat him. He lifted his head wearily, acknowledging her touch, and then put it back. Something was wrong.

Carole scratched his head where he liked it best, right on top. Usually this made his ears droop a little, as if to make more space for her to scratch, but this time his ears stayed where they were. Carole was concerned and decided to watch him carefully.

She returned to her knitting. She'd finished another inch of the foot when Snowball rose slightly and then began making strange sounds, as if he was coughing and trying to bring something up. Then he stopped the coughing and settled back down again.

That settled it. Carole decided to get hold of the veterinarian, Judy Barker. Judy was primarily an equine veterinarian, but she also looked after the other animals around her clients' barns, and that always included cats. Judy had known Snowball since he'd been born and she would know what to do.

Carole looked up Judy's number and telephoned her. Judy answered on the first ring. Much to Carole's surprise, she found herself talking to the vet on her car phone.

"It makes me feel so important!" Carole joked.

"You are," Judy assured her. "You are. So, what's up?"

Carole described Snowball's odd behavior and asked if she could bring the kitten into Judy's clinic.

"Sure you can, Carole, but actually, I'm only about three minutes from your house. Why don't I save you some time and worry and come by and take a look at Snowball now?"

"You'd do that?"

"Not usually," Judy admitted. "But my next stop is to see a horse who likes to kick me. I'd rather put that off a few minutes to check on Snowball. And besides, you're on my way."

The next thing Carole knew, Judy was pulling her truck into the Hansons' driveway and knocking on the door. Carole let her in and brought her upstairs to where Snowball still lay.

Judy patted the black kitten reassuringly and then checked him carefully. She took his temperature, listened to his heart, and looked down his throat.

"He's got a nice, long, smooth coat, doesn't he?" she remarked to Carole.

"Yes, he does," Carole agreed. "Sometimes it seems like he leaves piles of fur wherever he's been! It means I have to vacuum a lot, but I don't mind."

Judy smiled. "Well, this is a healthy cat. What's up is that he's got a hair ball, which is just a collection of fur he swallows when he gives himself a bath. He'll cough it up and that'll be it." Judy gave Carole some medicine that would both help him cough up the hair ball and help prevent him from forming another. Then, as they were talking, Snowball stood up again, jumped down onto the floor, coughed hard several times, and produced the offending hair ball. He looked up at Carole and his doctor as if to say, "So, aren't you proud of me?" and immediately began playing with the wool on Carole's father's sock.

"I guess there wasn't much to worry about, huh?" Carole asked sheepishly.

"No, but it doesn't matter," Judy assured her. "If an owner's concerned, I'm concerned. I'd rather have you call me when you've just noticed that something's wrong and it turns out to be minor than to have you wait until something serious is wrong and it's so wrong that I can't do anything about it. I wish all my house calls were as pleasant as this one."

Carole offered Judy a cup of tea, to help strengthen her for the kicking horse she was about to meet. Judy accepted gladly.

"Are you still thinking about becoming a veterinarian?" Judy asked.

"Oh, sure," Carole said. "Maybe, anyway. What I really know is that I want to work with horses. I just can't decide how. Maybe I'll just ride. Maybe I'll become a trainer, or a breeder, or a vet. As long as it's horses, I'll be happy." The pot whistled and Carole poured the hot water onto the tea bags. "Milk or lemon?" she asked.

"Just plain," Judy said. "Thank you." She accepted her cup from Carole and stirred her tea. "You know, if you want to be a vet, maybe you ought to get a taste of what it's like. You see me occasionally at Pine Hollow, and every once in a while at your home or in my clinic, but that's not the same as seeing me doing the rounds on all my equine patients. Would you like to do that some-time?"

Carole gaped. Then she realized her mouth was hang-ing open and she shut it. "*Like to?*" she asked. "I'd *love* to!"

"Well, aren't you on vacation now? Do you have any free time?"

"Just about seventeen days," Carole answered. "Minus the time it'll take me to finish knitting my dad's sock."

"Hmmm," Judy said thoughtfully. "I do emergencies as they come up, but my routine rounds are Wednesday, Thursday, and Saturday. Why don't you plan to come with me then? We could start tomorrow right after your Pony Club meeting."

"Wow. That would be absolutely fantastic!" Carole said. She was so excited that she banged against the table and spilled her tea as well as Judy's.

"You may not be so enthusiastic after a day or two of

it," Judy said. "If you're going to hang around with me, I'm going to work you hard."

"Working with horses is *never* too hard," Carole told her.

Judy smiled warmly. "Working with horses is often *very* hard, but always rewarding, so I don't mind, and I bet you won't, either."

"I *know* I won't mind," Carole said.

Judy had to leave then, but before she went, she made arrangements with Carole to have Colonel Hanson call her and confirm that it would be all right for Carole to tag along and give her a hand. Carole knew that even if her father had doubts about it, Judy could convince him. Anybody who could convince a horse to stand still while she checked his digestive system could certainly convince a Marine Corps colonel to give his daughter an opportunity as good as this one.

Even after Judy had been gone for a long time, Carole still could barely believe her good luck. She couldn't wait to tell her friends!

AT THE SAME time Judy and Carole were talking about Colonel Hanson, Stevie and Lisa were seeing him. He was at the mall.

"So this is the errand Carole mentioned her dad had to run," Stevie said. "I smell a rat, don't you?"

"Sure, but it's a Christmas rat," Lisa reminded her. "They're white rats and they tell white lies."

"We're shopping for Carole. How about you?" Stevie asked when Colonel Hanson caught up with them.

"Me, too," he said. "I have something in mind for her big present, but I want some fun little things to put in her stocking and under the tree."

"Her big present is so big it doesn't fit under the tree?" Lisa asked, impressed.

"Not the tree we're putting up this weekend," the colonel said. "And that reminds me that I've been meaning to call you girls. I can use some help here and I suspect you're the ones to give it to me. Why don't we leave all these boring scarves, fuzzy slippers, and earrings behind us, step over to Pizza Man across the way, and have a little talk?"

"I'm never too full of junk food to say no to pizza," Stevie said, leading the way.

In a few minutes, Colonel Hanson and the girls were settled into a booth, waiting as a pepperoni, sausage, and mushroom pizza was being cooked especially for them.

"So, how can we help?" Stevie asked, getting down to business.

"Well," the colonel began, "when Carole's mother died two years ago, she left Carole a small bequest, really a legacy from Carole's grandmother. It's been in a bank, collecting interest, and I've decided what I want to do with it."

"What's a bequest? And where do we come in?" Lisa asked.

"Pepperoni, sausage, mushroom special, piping hot, coming in!" the waiter said. He put the pizza on the center of the table. Then he dashed back to the counter and reappeared with their drinks, some paper plates, and napkins.

"Oh, I love it!" Stevie said. "A pizza with everything *I* want, and nothing my brothers want!"

Each of them took a slice.

"So, where were we?" Stevie asked. "Something to do with Carole's mom?"

CAROLE HEARD HER father's car coming into the driveway. She had to hurry. She didn't want her father to know she'd been up to something in her room. She folded up the nearly finished sock, packed it into her knitting bag, and scooted everything under her bed. She turned out the light in her room, went downstairs, turned on the television, and collapsed in the easy chair.

"Hi, Carole, I'm home!" her father called out from the hallway.

"Hi, Dad. In here," she said, staring fixedly at the television screen.

"What are you watching?" he asked when he came into the den.

"Oh, something on cable," she said, trying to sound casual. "It's very interesting."

"I bet," he said. "Looks to me like it's the latest farm report. Those can be spellbinding!"

Carole looked more carefully at the screen. Her father was right. An agricultural specialist was interviewing a farmer about the infestation problem on his soy crop. She was going to have a problem convincing her father she was interested in that! She decided to turn the tables.

"What have you been up to?" she asked, turning off the television.

"Oh, well, uh, not much," he said. "I stopped off at the Officers' Club. One of my old buddies—from before you were born—was on the base and I just wanted to have a chance to see him."

"I thought you had some errands to run. Did you get them done?"

"Errands? Oh, right. I stopped at the PX on the way to the Officers' Club."

The PX wasn't exactly on the way from her father's office to the Officer's Club, but she didn't pursue her questioning. Her father was definitely fibbing to her. She had the nicest feeling that the fibs meant he'd been shopping for her. If that were the case, though, where were the packages? She decided that he'd left them in the car. She also decided that she probably hadn't fooled him about the farm report.

Maybe Christmas wouldn't be so bad after all.

3

To Stevie, there were three kinds of secrets: good ones, bad ones, and boring ones. She had the best kind—a good one. But the worst thing about the best kind was that it was the only kind you really had to keep. Keeping secrets wasn't Stevie's favorite activity. Telling them was much more fun!

She dashed toward the stairs at her house, barely acknowledging the greetings from her parents.

"Hi, how'd you get home?" her mother asked.

"We ran into Colonel Hanson. He gave Lisa and me a ride home," she said.

"Dinner in a half an—" her mother began.

"I already ate pizza at the mall," she said, whizzing past both of her parents.

"Then you'll enjoy watching the rest of us eat—in one-half hour," her mother said pointedly.

"Okay," Stevie agreed. Some things weren't worth arguing about. Even though she sometimes hated being with her brothers, family dinners could be fun, if a little noisy. Besides, she thought she smelled tomato sauce and that might mean lasagna. She wouldn't miss that, even if she was stuffed to the gills with pizza!

She took the packages she had purchased at the mall and tucked them under her bed. That was her Christmas-present hiding place. It was also her lost-schoolbook hiding place, her missing-sock hiding place, and her broken-pencil hiding place. As a result, it was her cat, Madonna's, most favored hiding place of all. Madonna spurted out, chasing a dust bunny. She gave Stevie a withering look, and left the room.

Stevie tossed her coat toward her closet, slipped out of her shoes, and settled onto the bed. She picked up the phone and dialed one of her favorite numbers.

"Hi, this is Stevie. Is Phil there?" she asked when Mrs. Marston answered.

In a few seconds, Phil picked up the phone.

"Hi, beautiful," he said.

Stevie knew he was joking a little, but there was a part of him that wasn't joking and she liked that. Somehow, when Phil called her beautiful, it made her feel beautiful. It was a very nice feeling.

"Hello, hunk," she countered. Then she giggled a little. "Guess where I've been all afternoon," she said. "I've been at the mall."

"You're not turning into a mall rat on me, are you?" he asked.

Stevie thought about the girls she knew who spent every spare minute at the mall, window-shopping, or wasting their money on earrings and stockings. The girls in her classes who did that always struck her as very uninteresting, though very well-groomed.

"No way! I've been Christmas shopping. It makes me a sort of temporary mall rat, once a year."

"As long as it's only temporary. Did you have fun?"

"Oh, yes, lots. I was with Lisa. We actually bought some things for our families, too. You should see the mall. It's all lit up with Christmas lights, and carols blast from every amplifier in the place. You can't walk two steps without bumping into a phony Santa Claus or elves or reindeer. I'm really getting into the holiday spirit, aren't you?"

Phil laughed. "Around here, it's impossible not to," he said. "See, we're not just a one-holiday family."

"That's right," Stevie said, recalling that Phil's mother was Jewish and celebrated Hanukkah, while his father was a Christian and celebrated Christmas. "That means you get eight gifts for the eight days of Hanukkah, and at least one for Christmas—you lucky thing!"

"It also means that we've got Christmas cookies and

24

Hanukkah cookies, Hanukkah candles and Christmas lights. It used to confuse me a little, but now everything just comes in a great holiday jumble. I love it all."

"I always love this time of year, too, but my favorite part of all is the Starlight Ride. Did I remember to tell you about it?" she asked.

"No. It sounds terrific," he said. "Tell me now."

Stevie leaned back on her pillow and told Phil about the ride. She told him what it was like to be on a horse on a crisp winter night, with the stars above, and lamps to guide the way. "Sometimes, there's snow on the ground. I love the sound of horses' hooves crunching on the frozen snow. Sometimes it even makes me feel as if we lived a hundred years ago and horses are the only way we can get to where we're going. Horses are the only way you can get that feeling. I love getting presents, of course, and giving them. But the Starlight Ride *is* Christmas to me."

"Can guests come along?" Phil asked.

"What a neat idea!" Stevie said. The Starlight Ride would be even better if Phil could be there with her. Then it would not only be wonderful and Christmasy, but it would be romantic, too. "I'll ask Max. I bet he'll say yes."

"Ask him if you can bring two guests. My friend A.J. is coming over to our house that night, and I know he'll want to come. He's a better rider than I am, almost as good as you. He'd have a blast, too."

Stevie smiled to herself, accepting Phil's compliment about her riding, but not taking it terribly seriously. She and Phil once had wasted a lot of time arguing over which of them was the better rider and competing against each other instead of working with each other. Now, they simply agreed that each one would claim the other was the better rider. In fact, they were both experienced, good riders. They were good enough to have fun riding together and occasionally competing against each other. Stevie was looking forward to the next Pony Club rally at which Pine Hollow's Pony Club, Horse Wise, would compete against Phil's. She was sure her own team would win, but she'd die before she'd tell Phil that!

"Well, I'll ask Max tomorrow and I'll call you tomorrow night. Okay?" she asked.

"No, I'll call you tomorrow night because it'll be my turn. We're having a dance-committee meeting tomorrow afternoon, so I'll have lots more to tell you about the New Year's Eve party. The parents have been auditioning bands. I hate to think what they'll end up choosing for us."

Stevie listened while Phil described the trio with an accordion that one parent was proposing. Another seemed to favor an oompah band, and a third was in favor of a square-dance band.

"I'm sure they're all kind of interesting," Phil conceded. "But for a New Year's Eve dance, I want rock 'n' roll, don't you?"

"As long as the band knows a few slow songs, for, um, special times?" she said.

"I'll see to it," Phil promised. "Now I've got to go. I'll call tomorrow. Bye."

"Good night," she said, and hung up. She liked talking with Phil on the phone. It always left her with a nice happy feeling. If her friends had told her, six months earlier, that she'd have a boyfriend, she would have informed them that they were completely out of their minds. But it was true. She *did* have a boyfriend. And she *liked* having a boyfriend. Some girls she knew who had boyfriends seemed to have suffered total personality changes, and not for the better. Stevie had had that problem at first, but had come around to her normal self fairly quickly, and stayed that way, mostly.

For a few minutes after she hung up, she reverted briefly to her starry-eyed state. It was New Year's Eve. She was wearing a strapless dress of aquamarine chiffon, silver sandals on her feet, a diamond tiara in her hair. Phil, in a tuxedo, held her gently as they floated across the floor to the sound of . . . an oompah band? What was she thinking of? There was no way her mother would let her have a strapless dress. Phil would probably die before he'd put on a tuxedo, and if she wore silver sandals like the ones in her daydream, she'd have a broken ankle long before midnight. And as for the diamond tiara . . . No, the whole situation called for some serious thinking. Fortunately, she had good friends to help her.

Stevie reached for the phone again. She had to talk to Carole.

"You've been to dances at the Marine Corps base," Stevie began as soon as Carole picked up the phone. "Do you have to wear really high heels or can you be comfortable?"

"Comfortable!" Carole answered automatically. "Suffering for the sake of beauty went out with Scarlett O'Hara!" Then she continued without pause, "I'm so glad you called. Guess what I'm going to do! No, you'll never guess. You couldn't, anyway. It's too wonderful—"

For a minute, Stevie had the horrible feeling that Carole had found out about the secret. She gulped, and listened.

"Judy was just here. I wanted her to check Snowball—who is just fine, by the way—and we got to talking and it turns out that she wants me to work with her over the vacation. Can you believe it? *Me*, an assistant veterinarian! I'll be helping her with all her horse work and probably the small animals, that means dogs and cats, that she works with in her clinic, but the big stuff is the horses because they don't come to the clinic—she has to go to them most of the time. Isn't that fabulous?"

"Wow!" Stevie said, both relieved that the secret was safe and thrilled for her friend. "That'll be terrific. Think what you'll learn!"

"I know," Carole said enthusiastically. "Maybe I'll even get to do some things, like help her with examinations. I can do pulse and temperature, breathing rate, and stuff like that, because of what I learned from her and from Max already. How do you like the sound of Carole Hanson, D.V.M., equine veterinarian?"

"Equine? We are getting fancy, aren't we?" Stevie joked.

"Well, after all, it's the proper word for 'pertaining to a horse,' and it comes from the Latin word *equinus.*"

"You're starting to sound like a dictionary, or a horse-care manual," Stevie said, a little more sharply than she intended.

"Doing it again, huh?" Carole asked. This was a common complaint from her friends and, Carole knew, a fair one. "It's just that I'm excited."

"I know. I'm sorry. I'd be excited, too. Just don't get so excited that you think I don't know what equine means, okay?"

"Deal," Carole promised. "Anyway, we start tomorrow after Horse Wise. I can't wait to tell Dad."

"Haven't you told him yet? He should have gotten home about a half hour ago," Stevie said. Colonel Hanson had dropped Stevie and Lisa off forty-five minutes earlier, and Stevie knew that it was a fifteen-minute drive from her house to the Hansons'.

"How'd you know?" Carole asked. "That's just when he got home. Are you becoming some kind of psychic?"

Stevie realized then that she was on the brink of revealing part of the secret. There was no way she could let

Carole know about seeing her father at the mall. She had to think fast.

"Of course I'm not a psychic," she said as calmly as she could. "It's just that . . ." Her mind raced. Then it came to her. "It's just that *The Honeymooners* started on television half an hour ago and I know your dad never misses it."

Carole laughed. "You do know my dad well, don't you? It's almost over, so I'm going to talk to him now. I've got to go. I'll see you tomorrow at the stable, okay?"

"Right. See you then," Stevie said, and hung up, letting out her breath. That had been close!

Secrets were nice. Keeping them wasn't!

4

"LINE UP, NOW, facing me!" Max called out to the members of Horse Wise. Carole, in the lead, brought the line of riders down the center of the ring, stopped at the far end, and brought her horse, Barq, to a halt, facing Max. Stevie drew up to her left. Lisa came next. The rest of the riders did the same until all nine of the Horse Wise members were at attention.

"This has been a good meeting," Max said. "I think we're all learning a lot from Horse Wise."

Lisa thought so, too. In a way, the Pony Club meetings weren't very different from riding lessons, but in other ways, they were *very* different. Riding lessons, after all, were just about riding. Horse Wise was about everything there was to do with horses, including horse care, stable management, equipment care, and equine health maintenance. Today they had been working on tack, meaning saddles and bridles. They'd learned the different kinds of tack and what a change in tack could mean to a rider. Lisa hadn't really realized until today that a bit had to be the right size for the horse's mouth. She'd always thought one horse's mouth was about the same as another's. Now, knowing that the wrong size bit could hurt her horse, she was glad she had fitted Pepper's bit carefully.

At the end of the tack lesson, the Pony Clubbers had taken a brief trail ride. They had just finished cooling down their horses.

"I want to talk to you about the Starlight Ride," Max began. "We will all assemble here at seven o'clock. There will be an inspection at seven-thirty. All horses are to be completely and correctly tacked up, girths adjusted, and ready to go. All riders must have appropriate clothing, including hats, gloves, and scarves. Anybody who is not completely and perfectly outfitted will remain at the stable. A night trail ride is a treat, but it is also very different from the ride we just took. There can be no question of anybody delaying the rest of the group just because he or she hasn't taken proper steps to—yes, Stevie?" Stevie had raised her hand.

"Can we bring friends on the ride?" Stevie asked.

"If your friend is a good, safe rider, and can provide her own horse, yes. But I have to be confident that she can ride well enough."

"This is a friend from Moose Hill, the riding camp,"

Stevie explained. Lisa and Carole glanced at Stevie. Any friend Stevie was talking about from Moose Hill wasn't a "she." Stevie wasn't giving anything away, though. "This friend is as good as I am—well, almost," she continued. Everybody laughed. "And this person has another friend who I'm told is even better."

"Should be okay, Stevie, as long as these girls have their parents' permission and obey all the rules." Max looked at all of the riders. "That goes for all of you. Permission slips are available in my office. Horse Wise dis-*missed!*"

The Saddle Club dismounted and walked their horses back into the stall area.

"This girl from camp," Carole teased her friend. "Is *she* somebody we know?"

Stevie grinned. "Give me a break," she said. "Phil's bringing a friend named A.J. We're going to have a blast. Let's face it, the only thing better than a moonlight ride on a crisp winter evening is a moonlight ride with a cute guy, right?"

"Oh, it's a guy, is it?" Veronica diAngelo asked casually. The Saddle Club exchanged guarded looks. Veronica diAngelo was Pine Hollow's spoiled little rich girl, who cared more about her expensive riding clothes than her horse. She was not one of The Saddle Club's favorite people. Veronica sauntered past the girls, yanking the reins on the bridle of her horse, Garnet. "Not surprising you wanted to keep it a secret, though. He's probably a real jerk."

Stevie, Lisa, and Carole answered Veronica's remark with glares.

"You know, on a jerk scale—" Lisa began.

"Don't even bother," Stevie interrupted her. "Personally, I think she's just jealous, and when she meets Phil, she'll be even more jealous. Jealousy brings out the best in Veronica."

"Like that, you mean?" Carole asked.

"That's what I mean," Stevie said.

Lisa was glad to know that Veronica's thoughtlessness hadn't hurt Stevie's feelings. She was about to say so when Carole gasped.

"There's Judy! And I haven't even untacked Barq! I can't keep her waiting!"

Stevie quickly slipped a halter on over Topside's bridle, clipped cross-ties to the halter, and loosened his girth. "Give me the reins," she said. "Lisa and I will take care of Barq. You go on with Judy."

"You mean it?" Carole asked, clearly grateful for her friend's offer of help.

"Of course," Lisa said. "Get on out of here. There's a lame horse out there that needs your soothing touch."

"Go for it," Stevie added. "You're still coming to my house for the sleepover tonight, aren't you?" she asked.

"Of course I am. It'll be a Saddle Club sleepover, which means we'll hardly sleep at all, right?"

"Right," Stevie said.

"Your overnight bag is in your cubby, isn't it? I'll bring

it so you won't have to lug it around the countryside with Judy. See you later!" Lisa said.

"Thanks, guys," Carole told her friends. Then, handing the reins to Stevie, she left to meet up with Judy. Lisa and Stevie could see the excited bounce in her walk as she left them. They decided that doing a little extra work for Carole was definitely worth it to see her so happy and excited.

Together, Lisa and Stevie began the work on the three horses. First, they removed all the tack and stored it properly in the tack room, to be cleaned later. Then they groomed, fed, and watered each of the horses.

Lisa had learned early on that horses were a lot of work. In her opinion, anybody who thought riding just meant climbing up into a saddle, taking a ride, and then delivering the horse to a stablehand afterward, didn't really know what horses were all about. It seemed to Lisa that for every hour she spent on a horse's back, she spent two in his stall taking care of him. She didn't mind, though, because she was horse crazy. She liked everything to do with horses, not just riding—although "like" probably wasn't the right word for some of the tasks, like mucking out stalls. Still, mucking out a stall was an important and necessary chore, and it wasn't too bad.

It turned out that Topside and Barq needed fresh straw in their stalls, as well as the routine care. It took the girls a long time to do the chores. All the other riders had finished their jobs and were getting ready to go. By the time Stevie and Lisa got to Pepper's stall, they were quiet with fatigue. The two girls entered and began brushing Pepper's coat. Stevie worked on the horse's far side, while Lisa worked on the side nearest the stall door. Since Lisa was shorter than the high door on the stall, somebody passing by might not even notice the tired girls hard at work.

Veronica diAngelo certainly didn't notice them. She walked by the stall, and she wasn't alone. As usual, some hopeful friends trailed her, drawn to her by her wealth and privilege.

"Look," Veronica was saying to the girls, "if you want to be in my club, you have to earn your way in. The members of Equinus are special because not just anybody can be a member. Understand?"

"Oh, yes," one of the girls said.

Stevie understood, too. She realized that Veronica was still jealous that she hadn't been included in The Saddle Club. The girls had never asked Veronica to join for two simple reasons. Veronica wasn't horse crazy and she didn't know what the word *help* meant, except when it came to helping herself. Besides, the girls knew that Veronica didn't really want to be a part of The Saddle Club. She just hated being left out of anything. Obviously, Veronica had decided to start her own club. This could be the only chance The Saddle Club would get to learn anything about it. Stevie crouched down beside Pepper and signaled Lisa to do the same. Lisa crept around the horse, put down her brush, and sat down in the fresh straw next to Stevie. They both listened intently.

"What do we have to do?" the second girl asked Veronica.

"Simple," Veronica said. "All you have to do is to see that Carole, Lisa, and Stevie don't go on the Starlight Ride."

There was a stunned silence on the other side of the stall. Lisa and Stevie exchanged startled looks. Could they have heard this right?

"Who are those girls?" Lisa whispered to Stevie. "Do you recognize their voices?"

Stevie nodded. "Elaine and Diana. They're new girls. So new they don't know how awful Veronica is yet."

"They're learning, though, aren't they? Do you think they'll figure it out before they decide to ruin our Starlight Ride?"

Stevie shrugged, then put her finger to her lips. Conversation began again in the hallway outside the stall.

"How can we do that?" Elaine asked.

"Oh, there are lots of ways," Veronica said.

"No, that's not what she means," Diana said. "She means how can we do such a terrible thing to anybody?"

No one said a word for a few minutes. Lisa thought she could hear Veronica's eyebrows arching. "You do want to be in Equinus, don't you?" she asked sweetly.

"Oh, of course," both girls assured her.

"Well, then, remember who your friends are," Veronica snapped at them.

"I remember, I remember," Diana said quickly. "So how do we do it?"

"As I said, there are lots of ways," Veronica replied. "But here's what I would do if I were you. Since Max is going to insist that everybody be on time, you won't have to hurt the horses. Just make sure the girls are late. The easiest way to do that is to take their horses out of their stalls and turn them out in the big paddock on the north side of the barn. It'll be dark out. Nobody will spot them out there. By the time the girls figure out where their horses are, we'll be long gone on the Starlight Ride and I'll be holding the leader's torch. Don't you think so?"

"Oh, definitely," Elaine said. "And you deserve it anyway. After all, you're a *much* better rider that Carole."

"Really?" Veronica purred.

"Of course you are," Elaine replied. "After all, you have your own horse. Everybody's always a better rider on her own horse. You're one of the best!"

"Yes, I guess you're right," Veronica said.

Stevie clamped her hand over her mouth to stifle the laughter that threatened to explode out of her. Next to her, Lisa's face was bright red, deepening to beet-colored. Lisa began to rise. Stevie knew what her friend was going to do. Lisa was going to tell Veronica diAngelo exactly what she thought of her, and of her dumb club, and of her nasty pranks, and of her stupid admirers.

The last thing Stevie wanted was to let Veronica know that they knew exactly what she was up to. With an effort, she swallowed her laughter and yanked at Lisa's sleeve. When Lisa glared at her, Stevie shook her head vigorously. She put her finger over her mouth. Lisa eased herself back onto the straw.

"We'll have to get here early, won't we?" Diana asked.

"Yes, but not too early. You only have to walk the horses out the nearest door, there, and free them. That's it. You don't want to be seen by anybody, understand?"

"Definitely," Elaine agreed. "I don't want anybody to see that."

"All right, then, it's settled," Veronica said. Both Stevie and Lisa could hear the triumph in her voice. "Now, let's go to the tack room. I'll show you where Garnet's saddle is kept so that when you come for class on Tuesday, you can soap it and saddle up my horse for me."

Stevie and Lisa heard the clumping noise of three pairs of booted feet going to the tack room. The girls were gone.

"I can't believe it!" Lisa said indignantly, rising up out of the straw.

Stevie stood up as well. "You mean you think that a dirty, nasty, rotten, low-down trick like that is beneath Veronica?"

Lisa couldn't help giggling. "No, of course not. Nothing is beneath her. She's lower than a worm. But this sets a new record. So why wouldn't you let me tell her off?"

"Well," Stevie said, handing Lisa the brush she'd dropped in the straw and resuming brushing Pepper, "how about: Forewarned is forearmed? Victory is mine—I mean, ours!"

"What are you talking about?" Lisa asked.

"See, now we know what Veronica has in mind. If we told her we knew, she'd find something else to do, and it wouldn't be any nicer than what we overheard. But now we know exactly what she wants to do, so we can think up a plan to fix her. I'm not sure yet what it is, but it'll be good. And I can promise you that it will not only wreck her plot to keep us off the Starlight Ride, but it will also somehow cleverly manage to keep *her* off it, instead!"

"Stevie, I love the way your mind works!" Lisa said, truly admiring her friend.

"Me, too," Stevie said. "I'm always glad that I'm on my own team!"

5

JUDY BARKER PUT her blue pickup truck in reverse and backed out of the Pine Hollow driveway. Carole sat proudly in the seat beside her. Somehow, she felt very tall in that seat. Maybe it was because the pickup was old and built high up off the ground. Or maybe it was because being a vet's assistant made her feel very tall.

"First stop is a breeder-trainer by the name of Michaels," Judy said, checking her list. "He's got a mare that won't carry a foal. She's probably got an infection that'll clear up with some medicine, but until we know what the infection is, we won't know for sure how to treat it. While we're there, we'll be checking a mare who's due to foal any day now, as well as some horses with sore legs and feet."

Judy swung the truck out onto the highway and con-

41

centrated on her driving, giving Carole a few minutes to look around her. She'd been in Judy's truck before, but she'd never taken the time to notice very much.

On the floor, between them, was Judy's car phone. Everything Judy did was important, but sometimes time was the most important thing. Carole knew that in the case of a horse with a life-threatening illness like colic, sometimes a few minutes could make a difference. Car phones were a great help to somebody like Judy.

Most of Judy's medical tools were in the back of the pickup, but the cab held racks filled with empty tubes and containers, which were designed to hold lab specimens. A small cooler lay by Carole's feet. Judy told her that it contained vaccines for injections.

"That keeps the vaccine fresh and keeps the bottles from rattling around and breaking. Actually, though, I usually try to warm medicine to room temperature before I give an injection. The horses are less likely to notice that way." Carole had watched Judy give injections to the Pine Hollow horses many times. She wished her own doctor gave them as painlessly as Judy did.

Judy pulled the truck up into the stable driveway. Mr. Michaels appeared at the entrance and waved a welcome to Judy. Then he returned to the stable while Judy and Carole got the necessary items from the truck. Judy had a little case, which she used to carry tubes, sample containers, syringes, and medicine for each stop. She assembled the things she needed and they entered the barn.

Judy introduced Carole to Mr. Michaels. Carole liked him the instant she saw him. He looked like a man who loved horses.

"This old gal's the one that's giving me trouble," he said, pointing to a bay mare.

"Well, let's see what kind of infection she's got," Judy said. She asked Carole to check the horse's heart and respiration rate, handing her the stethoscope. Carole gulped.

She was going to ask Judy what to do when she saw that Judy was deep in conversation with Mr. Michaels about the mare's symptoms. Carole realized that Judy expected her to know exactly what to do. It frightened her a little, but of course, Judy was right.

Carole stuck the earphones of the stethoscope in her ears and put the other end against the horse's chest behind the elbow on the left-hand side. That was what she'd seen Judy do in the past. At first, Carole couldn't hear anything except muffled rumblings. She moved the head of the stethoscope around until she could hear better. There it was! The mare's heartbeat was strong and clear as a bell, lub-dub, lub-dub. Carole could begin taking the animal's pulse, but her watch didn't have a second hand. She had to have a second hand to figure out the heart rate.

"Uh, Judy, can I borrow your watch?" Carole asked sheepishly. Without comment, Judy slipped the watch off her arm and handed it to Carole. Carole made a note to herself to borrow her father's old watch with a sweep second hand the next time she came out with Judy.

Lub-dub, lub-dub, lub-dub. She counted carefully for a full minute, just to be sure, though she knew the faster way was to count for half a minute and double the number.

"Thirty-three," she announced. Judy nodded. Then Carole stood back and watched the horse, counting the number of times her nostrils expanded to breathe in. Carole did that for a full minute, too. The mare breathed in twelve times in a minute. That was perfectly normal. Carole told Judy, who jotted down the information on her patient's chart.

Then Judy began her own examination. Carole held the horse and talked to her soothingly while Judy poked and prodded. The mare was very sweet. She didn't seem to mind at all. Carole hoped that whatever was wrong, it wasn't serious. Such a nice gentle horse shouldn't have to be sick!

Next, Judy looked in on the mare who was about to foal.

"She's got a couple of days to go," Judy said. "She seems fine. Keep a close watch on her, though. Call me when her labor begins, okay?" Mr. Michaels said he would.

The next horse they checked was a feisty stallion. Judy clipped on a lead rope, held him with one hand, and drew the blood samples with her other hand. It only took a few seconds, and like the mare, the horse barely seemed to notice.

"I'll show you how to do this," Judy told Carole. "But I'm not going to start you on a stallion. They tend to be much more high-strung than geldings and mares. You're a good, healthy assistant. I'd like to keep it that way!"

Carole smiled. Judy handed her two tubes with the stallion's blood samples. "Mark the horse's name, the stable, and the date on each of them," Judy said. Carole had to borrow her pen to do it. She made a note to remember one of those next time, too. The last thing she wanted to be was a nuisance!

Carole watched as Judy came out of the stallion's stall. Judy moved the stallion up to the door of the stall, clicked off the lead rope, and backed out quickly.

"Never turn your back on an unfamiliar horse, especially one who has flattened his ears and showed the whites of his eyes," Judy remarked. "Don't give him a chance to hurt you. He might just be frightened enough to do it."

Mr. Michaels nodded in agreement. "Old Admiral here has done it more than once," he said. "He's got a nasty temper, but his bloodlines are impeccable and he sires the most wonderful foals!"

"Really?" Carole asked. She knew that horses were

bred in the hopes of accentuating the good charac-
teristics of their sires and dams, or fathers and mothers.
A breeder might, for example, cross a good jumper who
had a bad disposition with a good-natured horse who was
a mediocre jumper in the hopes of getting a foal who was
both a good jumper and good-natured. It didn't always
work that way, though. Sometimes what they ended up
with was a moody foal who couldn't jump for beans!

"Are any of Admiral's foals here?" Carole asked curi-
ously.

"Oh, sure," Mr. Michaels said. "Let me introduce you
to one. Judy, you should take a look at this fellow anyway
because I'm about to sell him and I'll want you to certify
that he's sound."

Judy and Carole followed Mr. Michaels down the row
of stalls. There, in the last stall, was a big bay gelding
with a dark mahogany coat and a lopsided six-pointed
star on his face.

"Oh, he's beautiful!" Carole said.

"He is that," Mr. Michaels agreed. "And he's going to
be a champion one day, with the right rider."

"Bring him out, Carole. Let's have a look at him," Judy
said.

Carole stepped into the stall and took a close look at
the horse. He took a close look at her as well. She
couldn't help smiling. He seemed so curious, almost pup-
pylike. She clipped a lead onto his halter and scratched
his face, right below his eye, to reassure him. He nuzzled

her neck. It tickled. She was having such a nice time with him that she almost didn't want to take him out of the stall, but Judy and Mr. Michaels were waiting. She clucked her tongue and brought the bay out to an open area in the hallway.

Judy made a thorough examination of the horse's soundness, running her hands along each of his legs, checking his hooves, and examining his mouth. She asked Carole to take him out into the arena and jog him around so she could watch how he moved. After he exercised, she checked his heart and respiration rate.

"Everything looks okay to me," Judy announced at last.

"I thought so," Mr. Michaels said. "I just wanted to be sure. The last thing I need is an unhappy buyer. I rely on repeat business."

That made sense to Carole. But one look at that horse and she knew that whoever bought him was going to be happy. "What's his name?" she asked.

"Pretty Boy," he told her. "At least that's what I call him. I don't know if the new owner will use that or rename him."

Pretty Boy. It was a nice name and fit him, but it wasn't what Carole would have called him. It wasn't special enough for such a fine horse.

Carole returned him to his stall, bolted it shut, and returned to help Judy give the inoculations to the other horses. Judy showed Carole how to put the alcohol on the horse before administering the shot and even let her put on the alcohol twice. That was fun, but it wasn't as much fun as trotting around the ring with Pretty Boy.

Soon after that, Judy and Carole were on their way, headed for another stable where, Judy told her, there was a lame horse that needed some attention.

"Ninety-five percent of lameness is in horses' feet," Judy said. "We all assume that things will go wrong with their legs because they're slender and they don't *look* strong enough to hold up all that body. That's partly true and it's one of the things that makes horses beautiful to us, but the feet are where the problems really begin."

The horse they looked at, a chestnut mare, was no exception. She had bruised the frog of her foot, which is the pie-shaped section extending from the heel to the center of the bottom of the hoof. It is the part of the foot that strikes the ground, and as long as it was bruised, the mare would favor that foot.

"Keep her quiet, no riding, for about ten days," Judy instructed. Then she handed the owner some medicine. "You can give her some of this if she seems uncomfortable. It's probably best to let nature do the healing, but she shouldn't suffer in the meantime. I'll be back to check up on her progress."

The owner was very grateful for Judy's advice and looked relieved that the problem was minor. Often lameness wasn't minor and took a lot longer than ten days to heal.

When Judy and Carole climbed back into the truck, Judy gave Carole some more information about the mare and her owner. "That wasn't a problem," Judy commented. "If that owner had more experience, he would have known that it wasn't. I'm not complaining, though, and it doesn't have anything to do with charging him a fee for the visit. I would always rather have an owner ask me to look at a horse when they're not certain that it's a problem than to have them wait until they know darn well that they've got a serious problem. A lot of the time, success in healing depends on early diagnosis."

Carole made a note to herself that whenever she was in doubt, she'd call the vet. Then she realized that she was already doing that. After all, when Snowball had showed the slightest sign of being ill, she had called Judy. Snowball wasn't as valuable as a show horse, but what a pet cost often didn't have anything to do with how valuable it was to the owner. Snowball was very valuable to Carole.

The rest of the afternoon sped by. Carole could hardly believe the variety of illnesses and problems that Judy had to cope with. Would she ever learn to remember the difference in symptoms among all the kinds of lamenesses a horse could have? Any loving owner should have a good idea of these things, even without four years at veterinary school.

There were so many other things a vet had to know, too. When was it appropriate to increase a horse's hay, increase his water, change his grain, eliminate his sweets, decrease his mash, throw out the mash altogether? It seemed to Carole that about a thousand facts and ten thousand questions were whirling around in her head—and all that whirling was exhausting!

"Ready to quit for the day?" Judy asked.

"Oh, no, I could go on for hours!" Carole exclaimed. "Who is our next patient?"

"I think *you* are!" Judy teased. "And my prescription is a good night's rest!"

Carole was sorry the day was over, but a little relieved, too. Judy was right; she *was* tired. "Okay, Doc," Carole said. "But I'm going to get that rest at Stevie's house. We're having a sleepover. Can you drop me off there?"

"Sure thing," Judy said. Carole slumped down in the comfortable seat and never even noticed her eyelids drooping closed. She was asleep before she knew it.

6

WHILE CAROLE WAS napping in the pickup truck, Stevie and Lisa were busy in Stevie's kitchen, which was noisy, as usual. Lisa was greasing the baking dish while Stevie counted out forty marshmallows. It wasn't easy to count forty marshmallows, either, because her little brother kept snitching them from the pan. Stevie threw one at him in exasperation. Michael caught it in his mouth.

"Hey, neat!" he said. "Do that again!"

Stevie opened the door to the dining room and threw a marshmallow as far as she could, through the dining room and across the family room. When he left the kitchen to track it down, she slammed the door behind him and secured it with the bolt lock.

"Alone at last!" Stevie heaved a sigh of relief and returned to her counting.

"I made the calls," Lisa told her. "It's all set now. I'm just waiting to hear from Colonel Hanson. He might call us here tonight to let us know." She measured the Rice Krispies and set them aside to wait while Stevie melted the forty marshmallows in a saucepan. Stevie stirred the marshmallow goo carefully and tried to concentrate on what she was doing. It wasn't easy, with all the racket going on on the other side of the kitchen door. First, Michael banged loudly, then he shouted. Then he yelled for Stevie's mother to come to his rescue. Then he yelled at Stevie's mother when she refused to help.

"Brothers!" Stevie said as she and Lisa mixed the marshmallows and cereal in a bowl. Lisa nodded. She knew just what Stevie meant, and even if she hadn't known from her own experience, Michael was providing an excellent example of what could only be called typical brother behavior.

They were interrupted by knocking at the back door.

"It's Carole," Stevie guessed as Lisa dashed to answer it.

Carole walked into the kitchen, sniffing appreciatively. "What smells so good?" she asked.

"Rice Krispies Treats," Lisa told her.

Carole grinned. "Will there be any left if your brothers find out about them?" she asked Stevie.

"Absolutely not," Stevie replied. "Which is why we are going to guard them with our lives. They can make their own!" She completed shaping the batter in the dish. "The only trick is, how are we going to get them upstairs?"

It took the girls only a few minutes to figure out a way. They took all of Carole's clothes out of her bag and hid the dish there. They left the clothes in the kitchen for the time being, since Carole didn't need them yet.

"Great!" Stevie said. "We get the Rice Krispies Treats upstairs disguised as tomorrow's clothes! We are *so* clever!"

Stevie unlocked the kitchen door while Carole held her bag as nonchalantly as she could manage. Michael, Alex, and Chad burst into the kitchen as soon as the lock was undone. The girls scurried up the stairs. They weren't going to be able to fool Stevie's brothers for long, but they were able to fool them long enough to get to Stevie's room and slam the door.

"Whew!" Stevie said, collapsing on her bed. "Now I know what it means to run a gauntlet!"

The girls took off their shoes and got comfortable. It was time to talk. It was time for a Saddle Club meeting.

"I had the most wonderful day!" Carole said. "You won't believe all the things I saw and did. I got to hold horses and help while Judy examined them, and you should have seen me at the first horse we examined."

"Don't you love the 'we'?" Stevie teased. "She left us this morning just an ordinary horse crazy girl and came back to us this afternoon a veterinarian!"

Carole smiled. She didn't mind the teasing. After all,

she *had* helped with the examination. She began to tell her friends all the highlights of the day.

". . . and then, there was this foal we looked at," Carole said. "He was so cute you couldn't believe it. He is only three days old and he's prancing around the foaling box, swishing his tail. It's only about six inches long. His mother never lets him out of her sight. She's the most attentive mother I ever saw. Anyway, Judy wasn't there when he was born, so this was the first time she was seeing him. She had to examine him and give him some shots. He didn't seem to mind. In fact, he didn't seem to notice as long as he was nursing. The tricky part was keeping his mother from being overprotective. I got to pat her. She didn't pay much attention to me. She was much more concerned with what Judy was doing to her baby." Carole was about to explain exactly what inoculations Judy had given the foal, and why, when the phone on Stevie's bedside table rang. Stevie picked it up.

"It's for you," she told Lisa.

Lisa took the phone from her and said, "Hello?" Although Lisa lived down the block from Stevie, and although she was very sensible—in many ways much more sensible than either Stevie or Carole—Lisa's mother was always calling her wherever she was for one reason or another. Carole suspected this was one of those calls.

"Do you think Mrs. Atwood wants her to remember her vitamins this time?" Carole whispered to Stevie. "Or maybe remind her to floss?" She laughed at her own joke and was a little surprised when Stevie looked puzzled. "That *is* Lisa's mother calling, isn't it?" Carole asked.

"Huh? Oh, *yes*," Stevie said in a way that sounded a little strange. "Probably wants to tell her about bedtime or something like that," Stevie joked.

"Uh-hmmm, yeah, um-hmmmm, right. Uh, pretty, right, yes. That's it. I think so . . . sometime next week, okay? Sure, Wednesday afternoon is fine, Colonel, of course. Bye for now."

Stevie glared at Lisa as she hung up the phone. Lisa instantly realized her mistake. The caller wasn't Lisa's mother at all, but Carole's father. Lisa had slipped badly by calling him Colonel. *How are we going to cover that?* Stevie wondered.

"You call your mother *Colonel?*" Carole asked, now definitely suspicious.

"Oh, not my mother," Lisa said quickly.

"Stevie said it was your mother who called. What's going on here?" Carole wanted to know.

"Oh, of course it was my mother who called," Lisa said, trying to sound as logical as possible. "But she called me because there was this Salvation Army colonel at our house and she wanted me to talk to him. I'm going to be doing some volunteer work for them over vacation, so we had to make arrangements. It's this new thing she's gotten me into. I'll tell you about it some other time. It's pretty boring, though. So why don't you tell us more about the foal?"

"Oh, right, the foal," Carole said, trying to remember where she had left off. "So, anyway, there I am, holding the mother, who wasn't paying any attention to me, when the owner asked Judy if it would be all right to let the two of them out into a little paddock right off the foaling box. Judy said sure, as soon as she was finished. We got to wait and watch. The owner opened the door up and the mare led the way. That three-day-old just gaped at the open door at first. It was like he couldn't have imagined something so wonderful and so frightening. He sniffed and cocked his head to listen. He took a couple of steps toward the light. I think he would have stood and looked forever if it hadn't been for his mother. She stepped into the warm sunshine outside and then began calling to him. He took slow, careful steps, sniffing, looking, and listening every step of the way. Then, of course, once he got outside, he was at home. After fifteen minutes, when it was time to bring them back in, he started acting like he'd found his new home and he didn't want all that indoor stuff! His mother was ready to go back in, though. She gave him a piece of her mind and a nudge with her nose. He got back into the foaling box, took a sip or two or milk from her, and then practically collapsed to take his nap. He was so cute. He was almost snoring!"

Listening to Carole was almost like being there, Lisa thought. She could see the newborn trying out his independence for the first time. She could even understand how he felt.

"It's a little bit like the first day of school, isn't it?" Lisa mused. "Going off on the school bus by yourself, just terrified. Then, by the time the second day of school comes around, you're a pro at it. You wave good-bye to your mother and that's that."

"That's just what it was like," Carole agreed. "For one second, he's too scared to move. Then, the next minute, he knows all the ropes!"

Stevie cut up the Rice Krispies Treats, now cool enough to eat, and passed them around to her friends. "Lisa and I had an eventful day, too," she said. "After you left, we managed to overhear a very interesting conversation Veronica diAngelo had with Diana and Elaine."

"Veronica actually said something interesting?" Carole asked.

"Very interesting," Lisa assured her. She and Stevie filled Carole in on the events planned in their honor for the Starlight Ride.

"Why, of all the . . . !" Carole sputtered. "I can't believe . . . How could she even dare . . . ?"

"Don't worry," Lisa said. "Stevie's got a plan that will get her but good."

"You do?" Carole asked.

"Not quite. But I will," Stevie said firmly. "Trust me."

There were things Lisa and Carole knew they could trust Stevie to do. Getting back at Veronica was one of them.

The phone rang again. This time it was Phil calling Stevie. Carole and Lisa knew it immediately by the sweet tone of Stevie's voice.

Stevie was glad he called. She'd been anxious to tell him what Max had said about having guests along on the Starlight Ride. She told him he was invited—without mentioning that she'd left almost everybody there with the impression that her friends were girls, not boys. Phil and A.J. had their own horses and would bring them to Pine Hollow in the same van that Phil had used to bring his horse to Moose Hill.

"Oh, great!" Stevie said happily. "Then I don't have to wait until New Year's Eve to see you. I'll see you next week on Saturday!"

"You'll see me before that if I have anything to say about it," Phil declared. "Tuesday is the first night of Hanukkah. My parents said I could invite some friends over. Would you and Lisa and Carole like to come?"

"I'd love to," Stevie said. "But let me check with the others. Lisa and Carole are right here." She put her hand on the phone and told her friends about the invitation.

"No problem," Lisa said. "As long as my mother—"

"I know," Stevie said. "I'll tell him yes. You handle your mother. Carole?"

Carole shook her head. "Can't do it," she said. "It's

the night that Judy has her small-animal clinic open and I promised I'd help her out. Maybe next year."

"You get two yeses," Stevie told Phil. "Lisa and I will be there. Carole can't come. She's working with our vet that day. Wait until you hear her stories!"

Carole was sorry to be missing the party at Phil's. She liked Phil and she thought it would be fun. Still, she wouldn't trade anything for the time she was spending with Judy.

Stevie finished her phone call and then got an okay from her parents about going to Phil's, bringing Carole's clothes up from the kitchen with her. Lisa would have liked to have checked with her parents as well, but she was afraid the phone conversation might remind Carole about her earlier conversation with her "mother" and the "Salvation Army colonel." The sooner Carole forgot about that, the better.

The girls finished the last of their Rice Krispies Treats and put on their pajamas. They weren't ready to sleep yet, but it was time to get comfortable.

Stevie's room was set up with two twin beds and a futon for the third sleepover guest. The girls drew straws. Carole won the futon and she was glad about it. She snuggled down into the covers and looked up at the ceiling.

Lisa and Stevie were having a lively conversation about possible ways to wreck Veronica's scheme. Carole was very interested in their ideas, but she found it hard to focus on what they were saying. Her mind was a jumble of thoughts from the day. She recalled every horse she and Judy had seen, and all their ailments. When she closed her eyes, syringes, sample tubes, leg wraps, and veterinary instruments seemed to dance before her, like the visions of sugarplums in the poem that began, "'Twas the night before Christmas . . ."

Her thoughts moved on. The night before Christmas was the night of the Starlight Ride. And the next day would be Christmas.

That would be the second Christmas without her mother. Carole tried to think of it in a more positive way. It would be the second Christmas she could share with just her father. She sighed. It was a nice try, but it didn't change the truth. She knew her father was going to love his socks, and she would love whatever he gave her, but it couldn't make up to either of them what they were missing. She didn't care about herself, but she wanted to make it all right for him. She wanted to make him happy.

Her eyes closed again and she quickly drifted into a deep sleep, dreaming of horses wearing argyle socks to keep their feet warm on a cold winter night.

STEVIE COULDN'T BELIEVE how much she cared about
what she was wearing. Usually, she was satisfied with
grabbing a pair of jeans up off the closet floor, and throw-
ing on any shirt that happened to be lying around. But
now, before going to Phil's with Lisa for the Hanukkah
celebration, she'd spent a full twenty minutes selecting
an outfit and another ten minutes deciding exactly what
shade of tan panty hose to wear with it. She looked in
the mirror to make sure it really was her.

It was. Not only that, but with a light application of
mascara and lip gloss, it was a prettier version of her. She
smiled at herself in the mirror. She thought she might
even look better by candlelight.

"Stevie, you're beautiful. So, let's go," Lisa said. Lisa

had watched the entire process. She had even approved the shade of panty hose.

The girls weren't exactly dressed up, but they looked very nice. Lisa was wearing a wool jumper with a turtleneck and low-heeled shoes. Stevie ended up wearing a kilt, a pretty white blouse with a red sweater over it, and red shoes.

"I think the red shoes are a nice festive touch," Stevie said.

"Nice festive touch?" Lisa asked. It wasn't that she didn't agree; she just couldn't believe she'd heard Stevie say it.

"I guess I mean they go well, huh?" Stevie sounded sheepish.

Lisa nodded.

STEVIE'S FATHER DROVE them to Phil's house. When they arrived, the Marstons invited him to join them for a little holiday cheer. For a few terrible seconds, Stevie was afraid that he was actually going to accept. Fortunately, Mr. Lake had the good sense to go home. Stevie and Lisa went in.

Stevie had already met Phil's parents, and she introduced Lisa to them. Then they met Phil's sisters. His older sister, Barbara, was sixteen, and Rachel, his younger sister, was ten.

Then Phil introduced A.J. to Stevie and Lisa. A.J. was Phil's age, but he was much smaller than Phil. He had bright red hair and a personality to match.

"I'm awfully glad to meet the girl who was able to teach Phil so much about riding this summer," A.J. said, shaking Stevie's hand. "He thinks he knows everything. I've been telling him he doesn't, but he never listens to me. But you succeeded! And for that, my lady, I owe you a great debt." With that, A.J. took Stevie's hand and pretended to kiss the back of it, just like a seventeenth-century courtier.

Naturally, Stevie curtsied. "But, my lord," she said, instantly slipping into character, "I make it my job to tell everybody that they don't know as much as they think they do. I think you'll be next!"

"Try it and I'll sic the dragon on you instead of slaying it for you, my lady!" A.J. retorted.

Lisa and Phil laughed.

"Is this going to be a long night?" Lisa asked him.

"Could be," he agreed. "But I've got an idea. Let's leave these two to talk and go check out the food. Wait'll you see what my mother's cooked for us!"

"Food? Did somebody say *food?*" A.J. asked enthusiastically. "Just follow my nose!"

The four of them went into the dining room, where a tantalizing buffet was spread out on the table.

"Mrs. Marston, this is just great!" A.J. declared. "But what are the rest of you going to have?"

Phil snorted. "Even *you* couldn't eat that much."

"And nobody's going to eat yet," Mrs. Marston said. "First we have to light the Hanukkah candles."

The dining table had a candelabra on it, but that wasn't for Hanukkah. The Hanukkah candle holder, or menorah, was standing by itself on the sideboard. It had room for nine candles. Eight of them were the same height. One candle, placed in the center of the menorah, was taller than the rest.

The whole family and their guests gathered around the dining room table. Mrs. Marston spoke. "Tonight, since it's the first night of Hanukkah, we just have one candle, the one farthest to the right, and the tall one, called the shammash. The festival of Hanukkah celebrates a miracle, recalling a time when the besieged Jewish tribe of the Maccabees had only enough oil to light their temple for one night. But the oil lasted for eight nights, showing us how we can rejoice in strength we have that we didn't know we had. Each night we light one additional candle, remembering the miracle."

Then Mrs. Marston recited a prayer in Hebrew. Mr. Marston translated it into English. After that, Rachel struck a match and lit the shammash. She used the shammash to light the first candle, put it back in its place, and stood back.

There was a moment of quiet. Stevie looked at the lovely glow of the menorah and its light as it reflected on all of the Marstons and their guests. Then, as if on cue, the Marstons began singing a Hebrew song. Stevie recognized the tune, but not the words. The tune was the same as a hymn she sometimes heard in church. The song the Marstons sang was called "Rock of Ages," but wasn't anything like the old Christian hymn of the same name. It was a much brighter and happier song than that one.

"Next stop, the table!" Mrs. Marston announced, showing everybody where to get a plate. She didn't have to show them where to fill it up. The table was positively overflowing with good things to eat.

"The most traditional Hanukkah food is *latkes*. We eat fried food at Hanukkah, particularly *latkes*, because they are cooked in oil," Phil said. "At Hanukkah, we call them *latkes*. The rest of the year, they're known as potato pancakes."

"But they're always known as delicious," A.J. finished, loading his plate with the pancakes.

"Don't take him too seriously," Phil said. "Food is A.J.'s favorite subject."

Lisa thought it would be hard to take anything about A.J. very seriously. He was too funny for that!

They filled up their plates and then took their places at a table Mrs. Marston had set for the four of them near the fireplace.

"There's something else you should know about Hanukkah," Phil said as they sat down. He looked a little embarrassed. "It has to do with presents."

Stevie smiled to herself. She had a feeling she knew what was coming.

"We give gifts on Hanukkah—not big, expensive

ones, just little ones," Phil continued. "Traditionally, it's something like a child's top, a dreidel. Anyway, I do have a little present for you, Stevie, but it's just because you're my guest. You shouldn't worry that you don't have anything for me." He gave her a small package, wrapped in blue-and-silver paper with little dreidels on it.

"Oh, I'm not worried," Stevie said. She handed Phil a small package of her own, wrapped with red-and-green paper and topped with a big red bow.

"Isn't this cute?" A.J. asked, batting his eyes at Lisa.

Lisa grinned. "I think so," she said. "So, go ahead and open them, guys."

"You first," Phil told Stevie.

Stevie looked at the box. She had thought so much about her gift to Phil that it hadn't occurred to her that Phil would give her something, too. Carefully and slowly, she broke the tape and removed the paper, unwrapping a small brown jeweler's box. She opened the box. There, lying on the velvet lining, was a small silver horseshoe on a silver chain. It was beautiful. It was perfect. For a moment, Stevie was overwhelmed.

"This isn't a dreidel!" she managed to say. Suddenly she felt terribly embarrassed about her little present for Phil.

"Well, you can spin it on the chain if you want, but I think you'll have more fun wearing it," Phil teased her.

"I think so, too," Stevie agreed. She took it out of the box and asked Lisa to help her put it on. Phil smiled as he watched her. Stevie made him take her to a mirror so she could see how it looked on her. He stood behind her in the powder room as she admired the necklace.

"Perfect," he said softly.

"Thank you," she told him, turning to face him.

Rachel poked her head into the powder room. "Is it time for the dancing yet?" she asked, wrecking the romantic moment. Phil and Stevie drew back self-consciously and smiled at each other.

"Not yet," Phil told his sister. "We have to finish dinner first."

"And present opening," Stevie reminded him.

They returned to the table and Phil opened his gift. Stevie had gotten him a silver tie tack for his riding stock. It had a horse head on it with the horse's mane blown back by the wind.

"It's meant to give you good luck at shows," Stevie said. "Maybe you'll get lucky enough to beat me one day!"

"I need it, as you know—both the tie tack *and* the luck. Thanks very much," Phil said. Since he wasn't wearing a tie, he pinned it on his collar. Stevie liked the way it looked on him. She knew he was pleased and she was happy about that.

"So, tell us some more about this Moonlight Ride," A.J. said, changing the subject.

"Starlight," Stevie corrected him. "It's the Starlight Ride and, hey, I just thought about something. You guys can probably be a gigantic help to us. Especially *you*, A.J., if you're as much of a troublemaker as I think you are—and it takes one to know one! What do you think, Lisa?"

"Absolutely," Lisa said. "They're just what the doctor ordered—or should I say banker's daughter instead of doctor?"

Stevie nodded and grinned wickedly.

"Do you have any idea what they're talking about?" A.J. asked Phil.

"Nope. But if I recognize the symptoms in Stevie, it has something to do with schemes, right?"

"Of course you're right. What else puts this gleam in my eyes?"

Phil and A.J. laughed, but they stopped laughing when Stevie told them about Veronica's plan to keep The Saddle Club out of the Starlight Ride.

"That's outrageous!" Phil said indignantly.

"But what an opportunity!" A.J. exclaimed.

"My thought exactly," Stevie concurred. "But just *how*? That's the question."

"How about we beat them at their own game?" A.J. asked. Stevie nodded. That was just what she had in mind. "Tell me," A.J. continued, "do you know what horses these girls will be riding that night?"

"Probably," Stevie said. "Max tries to let riders stay with a horse they're comfortable with. Not all stables feel that way, but Max finds it works at Pine Hollow."

"So what are the horses they ride?"

Stevie scrunched her eyes and furrowed her brow. "Elaine usually rides the bay named Bluegrass and Diana's been on the Appaloosa called Chip, for Chippewa."

"What horses do you usually ride?" A.J. asked.

"I ride Topside, a championship Thoroughbred bay," Stevie told him. "Lisa rides Pepper, a dappled gray."

"Hmmmmmmm," A.J. said thoughtfully. "These are new riders, right? Pretty green?"

"Absolutely," Lisa assured him. "If they weren't new at the stable, they'd never go along with this kind of prank just to be Veronica's flunkies!"

"Think they can tell the difference between two bays or between a dappled gray and an Appaloosa?"

"Oh, *my*," Stevie said, getting the drift of A.J.'s idea. "The famous old switcheroo?"

"Precisely," A.J. said proudly.

"Devious!" Lisa said in sincere admiration.

"But how are we going to protect Carole's horse, Barq?" Stevie asked. "After all, she's the main target, because Veronica wants to lead the Starlight Ride. And, most of all, how are we going to keep Veronica out of the ride?"

A.J. scratched his chin thoughtfully. Everybody watched him. "There are ways," he said. "There are ways. Trust me."

Lisa and Stevie had the funny feeling that that was exactly what they could do.

"Listen, we're going to have to get there early," Phil said. "Is that okay?"

Lisa and Stevie exchanged glances. "We have to get there early anyway," Stevie said.

AFTER DINNER AND dancing and singing, Phil suggested that the four of them go out to the stable in the Marstons' backyard and check on the horses. Phil had his own horse, a bay gelding named Teddy. A.J.'s horse, a gray mare named Crystal, was also stabled at the Marstons'.

A.J. led the way, walking with Lisa and talking animatedly. Stevie couldn't hear what he was saying, but Lisa was laughing hard enough to assure Stevie they wouldn't miss Stevie and Phil for a few minutes.

"Why didn't you tell me you had such a wicked friend?" Stevie asked Phil.

"Most of the time, we just keep him in his cell," Phil explained solemnly. "We let him out on holidays and special occasions that call for his brand of genius. Besides that, I was afraid you might like him better than me."

"No way," Stevie said firmly. "He's nice, of course, but he's no Phil Marston."

Phil stopped and turned Stevie toward him. The night was cool and clear. It reminded Stevie of the wonderful, romantic nights at riding camp last summer. Phil looked as if he was thinking the same thing. He looked deep into her eyes and smiled. Then he leaned down toward her—

"Phil! Stevie! Get over here, *fast!*" A.J. yelled. Stevie and Phil ran across the lawn and into the stable.

"Look!" A.J. cried as Phil and Stevie joined him and Lisa. "Teddy's gotten cast! We've got to help him up!"

Stevie took stock of the situation immediately. She knew that being cast meant that a horse was lying down so that he couldn't get up. It usually happened in a stall because his legs were trapped against a wall, or because his back was against it so tightly that he couldn't get enough leverage to roll over and rise.

Teddy was lying on his side with his feet up in the air, wedged against the wall. He was flailing furiously, but his work was only serving to worsen the situation. More than that, he was in danger of hurting himself with sharp kick or hitting his head or face against the wall.

"I'll get your dad," A.J. said.

"I think we can do it," Stevie said. "But go ahead, just in case. Got some rope?" she asked.

Phil, accustomed to Stevie's quick thinking in emergencies, responded immediately. He handed her several lengths of a thick, strong rope. Without a word, she and Lisa began working together. Phil stayed by Teddy's head, petted him, and talked to him, trying to keep him calm.

With Phil to soothe him, Teddy instantly ceased his flailing.

"This horse is a good sport," Lisa said.

"He and I have been through a lot together," Stevie

said, recalling a terrifying ride they'd shared at Moose Hill. "I think we built up a sort of mutual trust."

She and Lisa looped the rope around the horse's bottom legs and tied them securely.

"Ready?" Stevie asked. Phil nodded.

Stevie and Lisa backed off and each began tugging gently at the rope. The idea was to give Teddy enough help so that he'd be able to roll over and stand up on his own. Two girls were hardly strong enough to haul the entire weight of a twelve-hundred-pound horse, but they were strong enough to give him some leverage, or so they hoped.

Phil moved away a little so that he wouldn't distract Teddy or get in his way. He made sure to stand where the horse could see him, though, and cheered him on.

"Atta boy, Teddy!" Phil said. "You can do it!"

Teddy rolled forward a little bit. Lisa and Stevie took the opportunity to help him some more. They pulled gently, constantly increasing the pull, but doing so easily so that they wouldn't possibly hurt the horse's legs or hooves.

At last, with a grunt, Teddy swung his legs up into the air and over onto the other side. Lisa and Stevie instantly dropped their ropes and unlooped them as fast as they could. They didn't want to hobble the horse when he was ready to rise on his own.

Unceremoniously, Teddy shifted his weight again, this time onto his legs. His haunches rose. His rear legs lifted upward. His front legs found their footing and his shoulders lifted upward as well. Teddy was standing!

It took a minute to be sure that he was okay. A horse who had been cast for a long time could have some serious problems, but Teddy seemed completely normal. He looked so normal, in fact, that when Phil's father arrived in the stable, he put his hands on his hips.

"Is this some kind of a joke?" Mr. Marston asked. "There's nothing wrong with Teddy at all!"

"Not now, there isn't," Phil said. "Thanks to Stevie and Lisa!"

Stevie was pleased that she and Lisa had been able to solve the problem so easily. It more than made up for the fact that Teddy's trouble had interrupted a moment she'd very much been looking forward to. However, in Stevie's mind there was no doubt about one thing. Boys were nice, especially Phil. But horses were *important*!

"So, ARE YOU all ready for Christmas?" Judy asked Carole as they bounced around a back country dirt road. It was the day before Christmas, the day of the Starlight Ride. The two of them had been working together since dawn to take care of all the urgent calls so that Judy could spend a quiet Christmas with her husband, Alan.

"Well, I finished my dad's socks last night," Carole replied. "They're all wrapped. I bought the fun stuff for his stocking last week. After the Starlight Ride tonight I'll have to fill it and sneak it downstairs when he's asleep."

"I tried that with Alan's stocking once," Judy said. "We ended up bumping into each other in the dark. Now *that* was a Christmas surprise!"

"Don't you think two people is kind of a lonely number for Christmas?" Carole asked.

"Not if they're the right two people," Judy said. "But somehow, I don't think that's what you're really asking, are you?"

"Not really," Carole admitted. "It's just that my father is such a terrific guy and it's hard for me to make his Christmas as good as I want it to be."

"I bet he feels the same way," Judy told her. "I remember—oh, here we are," she interrupted herself. They turned into a driveway and saw the stable next to an old house. "I don't know these people," Judy said. "They called my office yesterday, saying they had a horse with a foot problem. Let's go see what we find."

Judy and Carole climbed out of the truck and knocked on the door. They met the owner, Mr. Alonzo, and he took them to the stable. Working with Judy, Carole had seen all kinds of stables—big ones, small ones, new and old, well-lighted and dark. There were stables made for two horses and stables made for eighty. She'd found tidy ones and messy ones, but she'd never seen one like Mr. Alonzo's.

Four horses were housed in a cramped, dark building. The minute she entered, the stench hit Carole's nose and turned her stomach. It smelled as if the place hadn't been cleaned in months. Of course, that wasn't true. A stable could smell unclean if it was left untended or inadequately tended for just a day or two. But horses needed to be cleaned up daily, and these horses clearly weren't so lucky.

Mr. Alonzo left to bring the patient into the paddock, where Judy could examine the horse's hoof in the daylight because there was no electricity in the stable. As soon as the man was out of earshot, Judy leaned over to Carole and murmured, "Thrush, I'll bet you anything."

It only took a few seconds for Judy to examine the hoof and confirm her diagnosis. She asked Mr. Alonzo to bring out the rest of his horses. It turned out that one of the others had it, too. Carole remained silent, but she was furious. She knew that the thrush infections were caused by the filthy conditions of the stable. It was as if Mr. Alonzo were deliberately making his horses sick. Carole wanted nothing more than to give him a piece of her mind.

Judy was calm as could be. She patiently explained to Mr. Alonzo exactly what he had to do to heal the problem and gave him all the necessary medicines. Then she told him what caused it and how he could prevent it in the future by mucking out all four stalls at least twice a day and keeping them dry at all times with fresh straw or wood chips.

"Why didn't you yell at him?" Carole asked when they were back in the truck.

"Because he's not my patient," Judy answered. "He's the care-giver. If I yelled at him—which he richly deserved—he wouldn't listen to me and he wouldn't take care of my patients. And that's not good for my patients. I'll bet you anything that the reason he called me is because his last veterinarian did yell at him. Look who suffered."

"There are some ugly things about being a veterinarian, aren't there?" Carole asked.

Judy nodded. "But it doesn't make me not want to be a vet," she said. "I love animals and I know the vast majority of my clients do, too. I'd rather spend an entire night pumping liquids into a sick old nag for an owner who loves her, than fifteen minutes checking out a Thoroughbred that the owner doesn't care about except for how much money he can earn on the racetrack. I'll take good care of them both, of course, but I get more satisfaction when there's love there."

"In Mr. Alonzo's case, I don't think there's love or value," Carole said.

"Hard to tell," Judy said. "It may be that there's only ignorance. I'll try to help him. It's the best I can do." Judy turned onto the highway and headed back to Willow Creek. "Now, it's time to help you. We'll grab a bite to eat and get you back to Pine Hollow in time for the Starlight Ride."

Carole had been so upset by Mr. Alonzo that she'd almost forgotten about the evening ahead of her. Judy pulled into a fast-food restaurant. The two of them went in and ate a quick meal that would hold off Carole's hun-

ger until the cocoa and cookies at the end of the ride.
Cocoa and cookies seemed like an odd thing to think
about when there were sick horses to be healed and igno-
rant owners to be educated, but Carole decided that fun
was important, too, and that included Starlight Rides
and cocoa and cookies. As they drove away from the restaurant she watched the countryside out the window,
now darkening in the winter afternoon, and thought
about what it would be like to ride Barq in the lead posi-
tion on the Starlight Ride.

Judy's car phone rang. Judy picked it up. She said almost nothing, just listened intently. Then, at the end,
she said, "I'll be there in ten minutes!" She hung up the
phone. Carole could feel the truck pick up speed.

"It's the mare who's about to foal at Mr. Michaels's,"
Judy said. "Michaels thinks the foal wants to come into
the world hind-end-first and that can be real trouble.
We've got to get there as fast as we can."

The holiday traffic was heavy as families drove to
spend the evening with relatives. Judy drove alertly and
fast. There was no time to waste.

Judy pulled up to Mr. Michaels's stable and hopped out
of the truck, leaving Carole to bring the tools she might
need.

Carole entered the stable a few minutes later, carrying
Judy's "birthing box." Judy and Mr. Michaels were carefully examining the mare, a pretty bay, who was walking
around irritatedly. Judy and Mr. Michaels both looked

worried. Carole knew it was going to be a long night and Judy would need all the help she could get.

Carole put the tool kit down near the mare's stall and returned to the truck. When it came right down to it, cocoa and cookies weren't as important as a foal's life. The Starlight Ride, wonderful as it might be, couldn't compare with the importance of a healthy mare and a newborn foal. She picked up the car phone and called Pine Hollow.

Max answered. Carole explained the situation and told him where she was. It wasn't very far from Pine Hollow. She was only about three miles away across some fields. But she might as well have been on the moon because there was nobody who could drive her there. Besides, she wanted to be at Mr. Michaels's in case Judy needed help. So she would stay there until Judy was done. Max understood, completely.

"You're at Michaels's place?" he said. "How interesting." He paused, then spoke again. "Look, you'll get here when you get here," he said. "If you're late, you can meet up with us wherever we are. If you don't make it at all, well, there will be another Starlight Ride next year and you'll still be the best rider in the stable, so you'll lead the way then. Now, stop wasting time worrying about this. Go see if Judy needs your help. Oh, and, Carole, don't forget to have a Merry Christmas."

"Thanks, Max," she said. She hung up and quickly returned to the barn.

"CAROLE MAY NOT make it?" Stevie said to Max. "How awful! What about later on? What about tomorrow? Max, how are we going to—?"

"Take it easy," Max said. "These things have a way of working themselves out, you know. Besides, if Carole's not here, you'll be the leader on the Starlight Ride."

"I don't want to be the leader," Stevie said truthfully. "I want Carole here!"

"Don't you have something more important to do than to worry about whether she's here or not?" Max asked. "I know I do. I've got to go check the trail to make sure the snow hasn't hidden it."

It irritated Stevie, but she knew Max was right. There *was* a lot of work to do. And if she had her way, Max would never know the half of it!

She left Max's office and explained the situation to Lisa.

"Well, now we've got more time and we needed that," Lisa said reasonably. "Cheer up, Stevie. It'll work out."

"Do you know when he's coming?" Stevie asked.

"He just said he'd be here later, maybe while we're out on the Starlight Ride. We should be able to get everything done before that."

"I guess so," Stevie agreed. "Look, Max told me the things were stowed in the closet in Mrs. Reg's office. Why don't you get what you can and we'll work on this until Phil and A.J. arrive. Then, when they get here, we'll handle Miss diAngelo and her flunkies."

Lisa agreed that that was a sensible plan. She turned hurriedly to get to Mrs. Reg's office and found herself bumping right into none other than Veronica diAngelo.

"What's the big rush?" Veronica asked.

Sometimes Lisa had time to be civil to Veronica. Sometimes she didn't. This was one of the "didn't" times.

"None of your business," Lisa said, and brushed past her on her way to Mrs. Reg's office.

Veronica checked the sleeve of her blouse as if to see if Lisa had left any dirt on it. Stevie gritted her teeth and ignored the incredibly rude gesture. She needed information from Veronica.

"You're here early for the Starlight Ride, aren't you?" she asked Veronica, trying to keep her voice pleasant.

"Not exactly," Veronica said. "I just came by to see that Garnet's Christmas present had arrived—her new stable blanket. She's wearing it now. Would you like to see it?"

Stevie said she would. Veronica led her to Garnet's stall. The mare was wearing a fashionably tailored blue-and-green blanket with Veronica's initials monogrammed at the flank.

"Nice," Stevie said. "I like the colors."

"They match my new riding outfit," Veronica explained. Stevie expected as much.

Stevie felt sorry for Garnet. It must be terrible to be a

pure-blooded Arabian mare reduced to serving as a fashion accent for Veronica diAngelo. Stevie wished there were some way to make it up to the horse. While she thought about it, she idly polished the brass plaque by Garnet's stall. All the stable horses had their names on the outsides of their stalls on plastic plaques. The private owners usually used brass ones that showed both the horse's name and the owner's. Garnet's read:

GARNET GEM
Veronica diAngelo

"Are you wearing your new outfit tonight?" Stevie asked.

"Of course," Veronica said. "The car's going to pick me up in a few minutes to take me home so I can dress. You're going to change too, aren't you?" Her tone implied that Stevie needed to.

Stevie wasn't going to give Veronica the satisfaction of answering that question. There was absolutely nothing wrong with the clothes she had on. They were comfortable and warm—even if they didn't match anything.

"I think Lisa needs some help," she said. "I'll see you later!" She waved good-bye, but what she was thinking was *Good riddance!*

9

"THEY'RE HERE!" STEVIE said to Lisa. Lisa knew she meant Phil and A.J. Stevie had turned over a brand-new water bucket to stand on so she could see out the window when she heard the car pull into the driveway at Pine Hollow.

"Why don't you go get them?" Lisa suggested. She shouldn't have bothered. Stevie was already out the door of the stall.

Lisa finished up the work that was left, spreading the fresh straw evenly and putting the water bucket back where it belonged. It was hard to think of a stall as being sparkling clean, but as far as it was possible, this one was just that. Lisa was pleased with the work she and Stevie had done. It was exactly right.

Lisa straightened out a wrinkle in the clean horse

blanket and hung it over the top of the door, covering the horse's nameplate. She returned all the work tools to the tack and supply rooms, slid the screwdriver back into Max's toolbox, and followed her ears to where Stevie was giving A. J. and Phil the grand tour. Their horses needed to be unloaded, but that could wait until shortly before the Starlight Ride.

Stevie was about to introduce the boys to the stable's youngest tenant, a colt named Samson, when the foursome heard the distinct sounds of the enemy approaching. They all dashed into Samson's stall and, much to the colt's amazement, hid in the corner behind him.

"I don't like this, do you?" a voice whispered. It was Diana.

"No, but Veronica says we have to do it. It won't be so bad. Besides, I'd just as soon not have those girls on the ride with us anyway, wouldn't you?" Elaine whispered back.

"Oh, I don't know," Diana said.

The girls passed Samson's stall on their way to the locker area where they would be putting their coats.

"Not a second to spare," Stevie said. "You boys go distract the girls while Lisa and I get to work."

Phil and A. J. looked at each other and shrugged. They didn't have a better plan.

"See you later," Phil said. He and A. J. followed Elaine and Diana to the locker area.

"The grays first," Stevie said. She headed for Pepper's stall while Lisa went to get Chippewa. It only took a minute. The horses gave them no trouble. They willingly accepted the lead ropes and obediently swapped stalls. In fact, Chippewa looked quite natural in Pepper's stall. Pepper seemed a little confused, but Lisa gave him a carrot to appease him. He munched contentedly.

Topside and Bluegrass seemed to nod greetings as they passed each other in the hallway. Bluegrass sniffed at the hay Topside had been munching. Then, satisfied that it was all right, he began munching himself.

It had taken them a while to figure out what to do about Barq. He didn't look like Garnet, so they couldn't make a switch. In the end, they decided to swap Barq with a pregnant mare of similar coloring. She was far enough along that Max didn't want her ridden anymore, but she wasn't so gigantic that Elaine and Diana would notice her size. An evening in the paddock wouldn't do her any harm. Lisa and Stevie swapped their stalls and the job was complete.

The girls met in the hallway outside the locker room and stopped to exchange high and low fives before they entered. It gave them time to hear a little of what was going on.

"Oh, I bet you're a really good rider," A.J. was saying. Stevie thought there was enough sugar in his voice to turn somebody's stomach, but Elaine didn't seem to mind.

"Oh, no," she cooed. "I'm just trying to learn. I'm not very good at all yet."

"But you will be. I just know it," Phil gushed. "You, too, Diana."

"Me?" Diana said as if she wanted him to reassure her.

He did. "Oh, yes. You've got a wonderful build for riding. Strong arms, long legs . . ."

Stevie rolled her eyes. This was more than she had counted on. She had to put a stop to this before it made her sick!

"Oh, hi, girls!" Stevie said, entering the locker room. "Merry Christmas to you!" Lisa thought Stevie sounded even more insincere than the boys had, but Elaine and Diana didn't appear to notice. "I'm glad you all have met because we'll be together on the Starlight Ride. Isn't it going to be the most exciting thing?"

Elaine and Diana agreed that it was going to be. Lisa sensed that they were a little uncomfortable, which didn't surprise her. They were about to play a horrible trick on her and Stevie and Carole, and here they were pretending to be nice and friendly. Since she and Stevie were right there, it also meant the trick was going to have to be played under their noses. Lisa decided to make it easier on the girls.

"Why don't we go check on your horses, guys?" Lisa suggested. "It's going to take us about fifteen minutes to off-load them from the trailer, isn't it? Maybe we should do that *now*."

Stevie and the boys immediately understood what she

was up to. "Great idea," Stevie said. "The trailer's out in front of the stable, isn't it? It's probably not a good idea to leave the horses so far away and completely out of sight of most of the stable. Let's go get them now. We can turn them out in the little paddock off the riding ring that's on the side of the stable."

Lisa almost laughed. Stevie was being anything but subtle. She was doing everything she could to assure Elaine and Diana that they were going to be far away when the girls pulled their little prank.

"See you later!" Stevie said, waving to Elaine and Diana. The boys waved, too. The four of them left Elaine and Diana to their tricks.

Teddy and Crystal were accustomed to trailers. They were off and safely turned out in the little paddock in less than three minutes. That gave the foursome time to stand on tiptoe and spy on Elaine and Diana through the windows of the stable.

"There goes Chip!" Stevie said as Diana led her own mount through the stable to the large paddock on the far side. The four of them could hear the horse's playful canter on the hard ground of the paddock as he frolicked to the far side of the hillock.

"Bingo!" Lisa announced, peering through another window to see Bluegrass joining Chip in the large field. Finally, Elaine turned out the pregnant mare.

"You mean to tell me that those two can't tell the difference between a pregnant mare and a gelding?" A.J.

asked, still not quite believing that their plan was suc-
ceeding.

"That's right," Stevie said. "I knew they would be too
embarrassed to check. Actually, I'm not sure it would
occur to them. Anybody dumb enough to believe all that
disgusting sweet talk from you boys . . ."

" 'Disgusting sweet talk'?" A.J. said, pretending his
feelings were hurt. "Why, we were just being sincere!"

"Hmmmmph," Stevie snorted. "So, if you're so sincere, tell me your brilliant idea about Garnet. Just exactly how are we going to ruin Veronica's Starlight Ride?"

Phil's eyes danced. "Come on, we'll show you," he
said, turning to go back into the stable. He and A.J.
stopped at the trailer to get their horses' tack and the
other riding equipment they would need. "This is A.J.'s
brilliant idea, but it depends a little bit on Garnet. Can
we meet her?"

"Sure," Lisa said. "I'll take you to her now."

As they entered the stable, Elaine and Diana greeted
them, full of talk about how they'd both forgotten something at home and had to run, but hoped they'd be back
in time for the ride. Everybody said good-bye. The boys
waved *very* nicely. Stevie glared at Phil. He laughed, and
finally, so did she.

Garnet was standing contentedly in her stall, sporting
her new Christmas blanket.

"I have to admit that it's a pretty blanket," Lisa said.
"Just Veronica's colors."

"And the horse is a perfect color for our plan," A.J. announced, clearly pleased.

With that, he set down his bucket of grooming gear, reached into it, and pulled out a can of shaving cream.

"This is a mare, not a stallion," Stevie said. "I don't think she needs a shave."

"It is now six forty-five," A.J. said, checking his watch. "The Starlight Ride begins at seven-thirty, meaning that any rider with sense will be here by seven o'clock to be completely ready by seven-thirty, right?"

Stevie and Lisa nodded.

"Okay, then. We will take some of this completely harmless shaving cream, and before you know it, Garnet will be in a terrible lather!"

"Oh!" Lisa said, understanding at last.

"You *are* wicked!" Stevie said in total admiration. "Totally, wonderfully wicked!"

While the girls stood lookout, the two boys sneaked into Garnet's stall. The sweet-natured horse seemed to appreciate the attention she was getting. The boys talked to her, patted her forehead, and rubbed shaving cream all over her chest and belly.

Within a matter of seconds, Garnet was transformed from a contented, healthy horse to a lathered-up horse. It looked absolutely genuine.

It isn't unusual for horses to build up a lather of sweat. Most horses get lathered to some degree, and many horses get lathered with only a small amount of exercise.

But a horse who gets lathered up the way Garnet appeared to be, just standing in her stall with a good blanket on, was almost certainly quite sick—unless, of course, it was just shaving cream.

"Perfect!" Stevie announced. "Now let's get out of here!"

Stevie and Lisa showed the boys where they could get dressed and leave their things. While the boys were changing, the girls checked their own tack, polishing here and there to make sure everything looked perfect.

"This may be the most wonderful night of my life," Stevie said.

"Just one thing missing," Lisa reminded her.

Stevie's face clouded. "I hope that old foal gets born safely so Carole gets here. I don't want her to miss the ride. I don't want her to miss out on all the fun we're having. I sure don't want to carry the torch for her. That's her job."

"Well, even if she misses the ride, we do know one thing," Lisa began. "And that is that—"

"Aaaaaaahhhhhhhrgh!" Veronica diAngelo's scream echoed through the hallways of Pine Hollow Stables, startling all the horses and astounding all the people—or almost all the people, anyway.

10

"THERE ARE THE feet," Mr. Michaels said.

"It's the hind feet, too, just like we thought," Judy said. "This old mare needs some help and she needs it now."

She carefully and firmly took hold of the two little legs that were beginning to protrude and pulled downward, trying to hold on and help.

When foals are born hind-end-first, they often cut off the oxygen supply from their mothers before their noses are able to supply it to them on their own. Every second counts.

Carole watched in rapt fascination. There wasn't anything she could do most of the time, although occasionally Judy asked her to hand her something. Most of the time she just watched and learned.

The little foal and its mother were working very hard

to bring it into the world safely. Judy and Mr. Michaels were working just as hard. This baby was another foal of the old stallion they'd checked the other day. The foal would be a brother or sister to Pretty Boy, the beautiful bay that Mr. Michaels was selling.

Pretty Boy's stall was across from the foaling box. He watched everything that happened, too.

"Remember this?" Carole teased him. He didn't exactly answer, but he did nuzzle her neck. Carole located the carrot supply and gave him one.

"One more, girl, one more," Judy said calmly, urging the mare. The mare seemed to want to oblige. This wasn't her first birth. She'd done it lots of times. It had just never been as hard before.

"One more time!"

Judy wrapped rags around the foal's legs to get a better grip on them and she resumed her tugging. The mare was lying down, trying to help. Judy put constant pulling pressure on the foal, tugging downward, toward the mare's ankles.

"It's coming!" Mr. Michaels said excitedly.

Judy nodded, but concentrated on her work. It was hard, physical labor. Even in the cool stable, a sweat broke out on Judy's forehead. Carole suspected it was from both physical exertion and worry. This was Christmas Eve. It was supposed to be a time for joy, singing, happiness, even merriness. There was a part of Carole that didn't believe that anything terrible could happen to anybody she cared about, horse or human, on Christmas Eve. But there was a part of her that also knew that wasn't necessarily the case. She hoped the first part would be right.

"It's coming now, it's really coming!" Judy announced. Then, while Carole watched, the entire foal emerged. Judy almost collapsed onto the straw after it came out. She recovered quickly, however. Her work wasn't done. She needed to be sure the newborn was able to breathe.

Quickly, she cleared the foal's nasal passageways and began rubbing the baby vigorously to stimulate its breathing. There was silence. The foal wasn't breathing!

"Come on, baby, you can do it!" Judy said, once again checking that the nose wasn't clogged. She rubbed again. Then, with a start and a snort, the little baby took in one great big, deep, lifesaving breath of fresh air.

To Carole's surprise, she felt a tear run down her cheek. She hadn't even known she was crying.

"Nice work, Doc," Mr. Michaels said. "You got me a healthy foal!"

Judy finished rubbing the moisture off the foal. "I hope you wanted a girl, because this old lady's just delivered you a filly."

Then she stepped back and let the mare sniff her own baby. It was time for them to get acquainted.

Judy leaned against the wall of the foaling box, relaxing for the first time in more than an hour. She looked proudly at the newborn and her mother.

"It never changes," Judy said. "It's wonderful every time." She signed contentedly. Then, as if on cue, the beeper on her belt began whining. She glanced down at the display.

"The call's from Pine Hollow," she said, recognizing the number. "It's the phone in the stable." Judy looked at Mr. Michaels. "Can I use your phone here to see what this is about?" she asked.

"Of course," he said.

Judy reached for the phone and punched in the number.

Carole could hear the shrieking at the other end of the phone from where she stood. She couldn't imagine what was going on.

"Well, what does Max say?" Judy asked. "Oh, of course, he's out checking the trail. Is Mrs. Reg with him? . . . All right, all right. What about fever, pulse, respiration, those things, Veronica? . . . How can you not—? All right. Look, I can't come right now, but I'll send my assistant, okay? I'll be there as soon as I can myself, but I'm on an emergency here. . . . Doesn't sound like it to me, Veronica. I saw Garnet earlier today and she was fine. . . . I'll be there as soon as I can."

Judy hung up the phone. There was a puzzled look on her face. "I guess you heard," she said. "There's something wrong with Garnet. Veronica's too irrational for me to make much sense out of it, but since she seems to have forgotten how to check a horse's vital signs—oh, listen to me. I don't want to complain. It's Christmas Eve and it's not Garnet's fault that Mr. diAngelo selected her for Veronica. Carole, can you go check out the situation and call me back here if there is a real emergency? I can't leave the mare and foal just yet. There's still some watching to do."

"I'd be glad to, Judy. One problem, though. How am I going to get there?"

Judy started laughing. "You're so grown-up sometimes that I forget you aren't an adult. I was going to offer you the truck."

"I can't leave here, either," Mr. Michaels said. "But I've got an idea. If you can't drive, why don't you ride?"

"A horse?" Carole asked.

"Either that or a bicycle," he said, smiling. "But I think the bike would be awfully bumpy over the fields this time of year. Sure, a horse. I've heard about you, Carole Hanson. Everybody around here has. You're the girl who's going to be a champion one day. You can certainly ride a horse across a couple of fields over to Pine Hollow, can't you?"

Carole nodded. "Sure I can," she said. Then she thought about the most exciting part. "But which horse should I take?" she asked, holding her breath while she waited for the answer.

"Seems to me that one there, Pretty Boy, has taken a shine to you. Want to try him?"

"You bet I do!" Carole said. "I'll take good care of him,

too. I know you're about to sell him. I'll make sure that the new owner has nothing to complain about."

"I know you will," Mr. Michaels said warmly. "Here, I'll show you the tack to take. It's an old saddle, but it's the one I've been using for training. He's familiar with it."

It took a few minutes for Mr. Michaels and Carole to tack up the horse. Mr. Michaels explained that Pretty Boy wasn't fully trained and he might give her some trouble. "I'm sure you're a good enough rider to handle it, though. Most of the time, if he acts up a bit, it's because he's the one who's scared. Just show him he doesn't need to be."

"He'll never need to be scared with me," Carole said. Soon she had mounted the big bay with the lopsided star and was ready to leave. Judy loaned her a stethoscope and checked to be sure she knew the way. That was no problem. The fields were familiar to Carole. She wasn't at all concerned about that. She was more concerned about Garnet.

"I'll call you when I get there," Carole said. "After I check Garnet."

Mr. Michaels jotted his phone number down on a piece of paper, handed it to her, and opened the rear door of the stable to let her out into the starry, cold night.

The last thing she heard from Mr. Michaels's stable was loud warm laughter. She thought that probably meant that the little foal was trying to stand up and get something to drink.

IT WAS SEVEN o'clock and all was well, Stevie felt. In fact, things were going just perfectly. Veronica was hysterical, Elaine and Diana's horses were in the field, Phil and A.J. were saddling up. It was time for Lisa and her to do the same. She collected Topside's tack from the tack room and proceeded to Bluegrass's stall, where Topside was temporarily residing.

She had slipped the bit into his mouth and was just buckling Topside's bridle when Elaine came by, carrying Bluegrass's tack.

"What are you doing?" Elaine asked.

"Tacking up my horse," Stevie said sweetly.

"This is *my* horse!" Elaine protested. "Go tack up your own horse—if you can find him!"

"Oh, but this *is* my horse. This is Topside. He's the horse I always ride."

The look on Elaine's face was definitely confused. "But then where's . . . ?"

Stevie loved every single second of it.

CAROLE LOVED RIDING Pretty Boy. He was very tall and strong. A horse's height usually didn't say much about the kind of horse he was, but Carole liked the feeling of being high off the ground. She also liked his strength. She could sense it in his movement and in his response to her signals. As soon as she put any leg on him, he spurted forward, responding immediately.

"Whoa, there, Pretty Boy," she said. "We're just walking out here tonight. Maybe a fast walk, but a walk. The ground's too hard and unpredictable for us to do anything else. Just a walk."

With every word she spoke, the horse's ears flicked around attentively. To Carole, that was always a good sign. It meant the horse was alert and receptive.

It was fully dark out now. It was cold and the snow, which had been falling since early afternoon, tapered off, leaving a blanket of white on the Virginia countryside. The velvet black sky was studded with stars, and on the horizon the moon was beginning to rise. Carole had been looking forward to Pine Hollow's Starlight Ride for a long time. Now, she was finding that she was on her very own Starlight Ride and maybe even liked it better.

A cool breeze lifted a swirl of snow from the ground. Pretty Boy flinched and backed up. "Take it easy," Carole said, putting some pressure on him to get him to go forward. "That's just the wind. There'll be more of it before we get where we're going. Hold on there and go straight ahead now." The horse stood still. Carole put more pressure on him and then tapped him with her crop. He got the message and was soon headed straight for Pine Hollow.

"WHERE'S CHIPPEWA?" DIANA whined. "What did you

do with him?" she demanded. She stood outside Chip's stall with her hands on her hips, glaring at Lisa.

"Chippewa?" Lisa said in her most innocent tone. "Oh, I just thought he could do with a change of scenery for a few hours. Chip and Pepper swapped stalls. I'm sure you'll find Chip right in Pepper's stall, happy as a clam."

Diana gave Lisa a hard stare. Then she spun around on her heel and shouted at the top of her voice, "*Veroni-caaaaa!*"

Lisa almost felt sorry for her. Almost.

Stevie was glad that Bluegrass's stall was so near Garnet's. She and Phil were in there, tacking up Topside, when the plot unfolded to their complete satisfaction.

"Veronica diAngelo, look what you made happen!" Diana hollered as she and Elaine furiously cornered Veronica in Garnet's stall. Veronica was waiting for Judy's arrival to diagnose her horse's mysterious lathering.

"What are you talking about?" Veronica asked, totally confused and very irritated. In Veronica's book, tantrums were just fine, as long as she was the one having them.

"I'm talking about your lousy ideas! You made me and Elaine put our own horses out in the paddock!"

"*I* made you do something that dumb?" she asked. Her voice rose. "Do you really think I would want to have friends of mine make a mistake like *that*?" The scorn in Veronica's voice was obvious. It was apparent to Elaine and Diana that Veronica considered this failure an indicator that they were not Equinus material.

"I don't want to be in your stupid old club anyway!" Elaine cried. "You're just plain mean, Veronica. You planned this whole thing to make us look bad!"

"Veronica's mean, all right," Stevie told Phil, "but she's nowhere near clever enough to come up with a scheme like that! Elaine's just flattering Veronica!"

Phil laughed.

"Well," Veronica said, pulling herself to her fullest height. "It's a good thing you don't want to be in the club because I meant to tell you that the members had a meeting this afternoon and both of you were voted down for membership anyway. Too bad," she said nastily, dismissing them both. There was clearly nothing left for the girls to say. They didn't have horses to ride and they hadn't gotten into Veronica's club. There was no point in staying.

"Let's call my mom and have her pick us up," Diana said. Elaine agreed.

"I'd rather be home for Christmas Eve anyway."

The two girls left.

Veronica, unaware that Stevie and Phil had been listening, began playing out her own drama. Her face became distorted with fury. She wasn't mad at Elaine and Diana. She didn't even seem particularly worried about Garnet and her mysterious disease. She was just angry that her plans hadn't worked out. She began kicking at the straw.

"Oh, dear," Stevie said, approaching her now, "I hope you don't get that stunning new riding outfit dirty."

"You like it?" Veronica stopped kicking, suddenly attentive. A compliment could always get her attention.

"Oh, sure," Stevie said. "It makes you look just like your horse."

That was the last straw. Veronica's face turned a bright red. She was too enraged to speak. Without a word, Veronica marched straight out the stable door and slammed it loudly behind her. She was gone and Stevie would have bet everything under her Christmas tree that they wouldn't see Veronica again that night.

"Nice going!" A.J. said, emerging from behind a pillar where he'd been hiding for the show. He shook Stevie's hand. "I really liked your finishing touch there, Stevie. She looks like her horse! All *right!*"

Lisa, too, came out from the shadows, holding a fully tacked-up Pepper by his reins.

The P.A. crackled to life. "Inspection for the Starlight Ride will be in the indoor ring in five minutes. Prepare to ride!" Max's voice said.

Lisa, Stevie, A.J., and Phil were ready. Their saddles were shined, their coats were warm. They each had a flashlight. Only one thing was missing: Carole.

Lisa and Stevie looked at each other. The same question was on both of their minds. Would she make it in time?

"HERE WE GO, boy," Carole said, leaning forward for a final time to unlatch a gate and let herself into the big paddock by the Pine Hollow barn. She locked it behind her and turned to head for the stable. She was surprised when she spotted three horses wearing winter blankets standing in the far corner of the large paddock. It seemed odd that horses would be turned out into the snowy paddock at this time of year and at this hour of the day. There had to be some kind of mistake.

She needed to see Garnet, but she didn't have to get there in such a rush that she would endanger three other horses in the process. Carole rode over to where the threesome was standing peacefully in the field. She clucked her tongue to get their attention. They all looked up at her and then at Pretty Boy. Carole recognized the three horses and when she saw who they were, she was doubly confused. Two of them were due to go out on the Starlight Ride. The other was a pregnant mare who'd be better off in her stall.

Carole rode Pretty Boy around behind the threesome and began driving them toward the stable in the manner she'd learned when herding cattle on her friend Kate Devine's dude ranch. The horses obediently headed for the stable.

Carole reached down from the saddle, unlatching the stable door from atop Pretty Boy. The three horses had had enough fresh air and seemed only too happy to be home. Carole dismounted, fastened Pretty Boy's reins to a nearby pole, and quickly led each of the horses to its own stall.

All of Pine Hollow was aflutter with pre-Starlight Ride activity. There were young riders all over the place. Carole didn't stop to ask anybody what the horses had been doing in the paddock. There would be time for that later. Now, it was more important to look at Garnet.

"Starlight Ride inspection in three minutes!" Max announced on the P.A.

Maybe, just maybe, Carole told herself. But Garnet came first.

She put Pretty Boy in the empty stall next to Garnet's and then began to consider the mare's condition.

The horse seemed just fine except for all the lather. It was odd that she'd build up a lather like that standing in her stall, and it was even odder that it would remain there as long as it had. Carole checked her watch. It had been more than a half hour since Veronica's call.

Carole checked Garnet's vital signs. The horse's respiration rate was normal. She didn't look feverish; feverish horses usually looked droopy, like feverish people. Carole decided to check the mare's heart rate. She put the stethoscope in her ears and held the other end against the horse's chest, behind Garnet's left elbow. She had to wipe away some of the lather to do it.

The heart rate was completely normal. Carole took off the stethoscope and thought for a minute, rubbing her fingers together as she did so. Her fingers felt sticky and soapy. Horses' lather wasn't soapy; it was sweaty. There was only one conclusion. This wasn't regular horse lather.

Carole sniffed at her fingers where there was a residue of lather. It smelled vaguely soapy, too, vaguely masculine, vaguely like her father smelled right after he shaved, in fact.

Then Carole heard one of her favorite sounds. She heard the unmistakable giggling of her two best friends. She turned around. There were Lisa and Stevie, A.J. and Phil. Carole recognized the signs of one of Stevie's schemes. Lisa and Stevie were trying to control their giggles before they became outright laughter. Phil and A.J. were just grinning like cats who had recently consumed very fat canaries.

"I think I'd better check the calendar," Carole said. "Is this Christmas Eve or April Fools' Day?"

Stevie brought two damp cloths into Garnet's stall. She handed one to Carole and began wiping off the lather with the other. Carole pitched in.

"You should have seen it!" Stevie began. Then, in a jumble, all four of them tried to tell Carole what had happened. By the time Garnet was cleaned up to her normal, very healthy self, Carole knew everything, and was giggling just as much as her friends were.

"I wish I had been here," she said. "But wait until I tell

you about the foal that was born at Mr. Michaels's stable."

"Is *that* where you were?" Lisa asked, very surprised.

"Yes, and he's the nicest guy, and wait until I tell you how I got here from there!"

"Carole, there you are!" Max called out. "Come on, now, it's time for inspection. Is Barq all saddled up?"

Carole had the feeling that the less Max knew about Garnet's "lather," the better. She decided not to mention it at all.

"Actually, I haven't even seen Barq yet. I came in the back way on horseback from Mr. Michaels's stable. If it's okay with you and with him, I'd just as soon keep riding his horse. He's a real beauty named Pretty Boy."

"Pretty Boy?" Max said. "You're riding a horse named *Pretty Boy*?"

"I know, it's a funny name, but he's a nice horse and I'd like to ride him again tonight. Mr. Michaels is about to sell him. I want to ride him one more time. Can I?" Carole looked at her friends, who were staring at her as if she'd just sprouted another head. "Is something wrong?" she asked.

Stevie spoke first. "Oh, it just surprises us that you'd rather ride that strange horse than a nice horse like Barq. But it's okay. Barq probably won't mind, right Max?"

"I'm sure he'll be glad for a little peace and quiet. Now, how many times do I have to tell you all that it's time for the Starlight Ride inspection? Get on your horses and in the ring and sit tall in the saddles for inspection. Now!"

Stevie, Lisa, A.J., and Phil all headed for the ring. Carole had to call Judy and Mr. Michaels first. She explained it to Max. He gave his okay, but told her to hurry.

Judy was relieved to hear that Garnet was all right. Carole didn't want to explain about the practical joke, so it was a good thing Judy didn't ask for details. The vet was fairly accustomed to Veronica's hysterical outbursts about nothing.

Mr. Michaels was very enthusiastic about Carole riding Pretty Boy on the Starlight Ride. He was sure Max could board him for the night and didn't seem concerned about when the horse would get back to Mr. Michaels's place. So, finally, everything was set. It was finally time for the Starlight Ride.

11

"LET'S GO!" STEVIE told Carole. She was ready. Everybody was ready. Everybody had passed Max's inspection. Jackets were zipped, scarves wrapped. It was time to begin.

Carole led the procession out the door of the stable, where each rider paused to touch the good-luck horseshoe. It was an automatic gesture, but one that had come to mean something special to all of Pine Hollow's riders. Nobody who touched the horseshoe had ever been seriously hurt. Tonight, riding in the dark, it seemed especially important.

Max rolled the stable doors open and Carole, riding Pretty Boy, stepped out into the night. Max handed her the leader's torch and they were ready.

The trail wound through the fields and into the forest,

circling the hills that rose behind Pine Hollow. All the way, it was marked by bright lanterns every ten yards or so, so there was no way they could get lost. Eventually, the trail would end up along a small back road that led to the center of town. It was about two miles to the town center along the winding trail they would follow, two wonderful miles of lamplit trail on a starry night.

Carole took a deep breath and signaled Pretty Boy to begin.

"Isn't it amazing?" Lisa said to A.J., who was riding next to her right behind Carole. "I mean, look at the snow. It's like a fairy tale!"

"This whole day has been like a fairy tale," A.J. said. "I mean, who could believe all the stuff that's been happening, and how perfectly it's all worked out!"

"And you don't even know it all, yet," Lisa said mysteriously.

"I don't?" A.J. looked puzzled.

"Nope," she said. "There's more to come."

"Oh, yeah, all the caroling and the cocoa, right?"

"That, too."

Within a few minutes, the train of riders was through the Pine Hollow gate and everything was going smoothly.

"I've never ridden at night, you know," Stevie told Phil.

"No? What about that night ride at camp?" he said, reminding her of the time she'd ridden his horse to safety, escaping from a barn fire.

"Well, maybe," Stevie conceded. "But that was bare-back and barefooted, in pajamas, at a wild gallop most of the way. I mean, now we've got saddles and boots, and clothes, and no galloping. I think I like it better this way."

"I agree," Phil said. He reached over and squeezed Stevie's hand. "Also, this time I'm with you instead of worried sick about you! That's much better."

They all rode quietly for a while, enjoying the beauty of the place. The moon had risen now. It was full and silvery, casting a gleaming light across the snow-covered field.

Stevie thought she heard something. "What's that?"

"What's what?" Phil asked.

"That sound." Stevie cocked her head and listened carefully. "*Bells?*"

"Yeah, maybe," he said.

Stevie turned in her saddle and looked over her shoulder. There, behind them, but coming up on them quickly, was an old-fashioned horse-drawn sleigh! In the seat, riding proudly, were Maxmillian Regnery and his mother! In the back of the sleigh was a big sack that looked suspiciously like something Santa Claus might use. And in the front, taking the place of the flying reindeer, was Max's horse, Diablo, who was proudly drawing the sleigh across the field. His harness even had jingling bells on it.

Carole signaled for a stop. All of the riders on the trail

drew their horses to a halt so they could watch the sleigh. Each of them had seen it in the storage area of the stable for years, but none of them had ever seen it in use. After all, they lived in Virginia, where it hardly ever snowed. When it did snow, it wasn't always the proper occasion for a one-horse open sleigh. But tonight was exactly the proper occasion for it. It looked wonderful!

"I think we're going to have to sing!" Carole announced. Everybody thought it was a fine idea and nobody argued about the song. They all burst into "Jingle Bells" and began riding as they sang.

The horses loved the music. They all seemed to pick up their stride and walk more proudly, almost marching. Carole and all the other riders waved to Max and Mrs. Reg as they slid across the field toward the forest.

The riders were still singing "Jingle Bells" when they reached the first farmhouse. There was a candle in each of its windows and, in the back, where there was a picture window, Carole and her friends could see a brightly lighted Christmas tree. A party was going on inside. The guests crowded to the windows to see the Starlight Riders and waved.

At the next house, which had a decorated spruce in the backyard, the whole family came out to welcome the riders. "Merry Christmas!" they called. The riders returned the greeting.

"Sing 'Jingle Bells' again," one of the children requested. The riders were only too happy to do it.

"I think we need a new song," Carole said after they finished. "How about 'Here We Come A-Wassailing,' only let's make it 'Here We Come A-Riding'!" They tried that one out and liked it as well.

Stevie enjoyed the singing and she liked hearing Phil's strong baritone next to her own alto voice. It seemed like all their voices echoed in the cold night, carrying for miles.

Now Carole led the riders up the hill and into the woods, where the trail narrowed, but was still lighted and decorated. The woods were silent in the winter night. Here, the blanket of snow changed the sound, making everything quieter. The forest felt close and friendly, as if it had walls to protect the riders wherever they went.

"O, little town of Bethlehem," Stevie began.

"How still we see thee lie," Phil sang, joining in. The rest of the riders took up the song.

When the carol was done, they all rode in contented silence.

Finally, they crested the hill, rounded the bend, and came to the little road that led toward the center of town. When the last rider was out of the woods and on firm ground, Carole told them they could trot.

Pretty Boy seemed relieved to be allowed to go faster. It was as if he'd been holding in all his energy for this moment. He broke into a trot immediately. Carole couldn't believe his gait. Every horse's gait is as individual as the horse, some better than others. Pretty Boy's trot was wonderful and smooth. He had a long, proud stride, and his mane lifted in the breeze. He shook his head with joy, it seemed. Carole laughed joyfully with him.

And then it was almost time for the ride to be over. The Starlight Riders reached the center of town, where there was a small park. They circled the park, trotting halfway around and then walking the final quarter mile to cool down their horses. Carole led the group into the center of the park. There, surrounded by a waiting crowd of family and friends, and anybody else in town who wanted to be a part of it, was the reason they were there. A beautiful, tall menorah stood next to a life-size stable scene, complete with real, borrowed animals. Now there were horses as well. Carole brought the riders to the stable and then began the ceremony.

Carole took the torch she'd been carrying to lead the way for her riders, and used it to light the shammash on the menorah. Then, Stevie took the shammash and lit five of the menorah's candles, since it was the fifth night of Hanukkah. Finally, Carole took the torch and put it in the holder made for it above the stable. Her torch now represented the star of Bethlehem, which guided the three kings to the stable in Bethlehem as the torch had guided Carole's twenty riders to the stable in Willow Creek.

Then the crowd of parents and friends began singing, "We Wish You a Merry Christmas!" followed immediately by "Hanukkah, O Hanukkah!"

The rest of the Starlight Riders dismounted and secured their horses by a truck with some hay the animals could munch while the party proceeded.

The party at the stable didn't last too long. It was cold outside! But, the riders were glad to see, their welcoming committee had remembered to bring the cocoa and cookies. The mayor had also authorized a small bonfire to warm them all. It didn't last long, but it was fun.

Then the riders prepared for the return to Pine Hollow along the much shorter route, by the road. They checked their horses' tack, mounted, and lined up. Carole raised her hand to signal a start. At the same time their horses began walking, the riders began singing. The strains of the riders singing "Silent Night" echoed through the town after them.

All the riders were quiet on the return ride. Carole was sure everybody was sad that the wonderful, magical ride was almost over, although perhaps not quite as sad as she was.

She leaned forward and patted Pretty Boy on his neck. They had traveled very far together in one short evening. They'd gone from a miraculous birth in Mr. Michaels's stable, ridden across cold pastures, rounded up three horses turned out into a paddock for a prank, examined a *very* mysterious disease of a certain healthy mare, and ridden through more pastures, fields, and a make-believe stable. Pretty Boy had been her companion all night and Carole was glad he had. The horse seemed glad, too, although she suspected he'd be gladder once he got his tack off and could snuggle into a warm blanket with some fresh water and feed.

"You know," she told Pretty Boy. His ears perked up. She was sure he could understand. "I'm awfully grateful to my friends for that silly trick they played on Veronica. Not only did it work, but it also made it possible for me to be here tonight, riding you."

Pretty Boy snorted. Carole thought he agreed with her and was happy about it, too.

12

"THAT WAS WONDERFUL, every minute of it," Phil told Stevie.

"Oh, the wonderful part isn't over yet," she replied, leading Topside to his stall.

"Here, I'll give you a hand, and then you can help me with Teddy," Phil suggested. "He'll probably behave better if you put him on the van. You really have a special way with him. I don't know what it is, but he trusts you."

Stevie shrugged. "I don't know either. I've only saved his life twice," she added slyly.

"Well, maybe that's it," Phil said, and laughed.

Phil followed Stevie into Topside's stall and took Topside's tack as Stevie removed it. With Phil's help, the work went very quickly. Topside was brushed down, blanketed, watered, and fed in a matter of minutes. Then it was Teddy's turn.

"We need to hurry a bit," Stevie said.

"Not too much, I hope," Phil said. "I haven't seen you alone for a minute all night."

Stevie smiled at him. It was true. They'd been so busy playing pranks that they hadn't been together at all.

"As long as we don't embarrass Teddy . . ." Stevie said mischievously.

"He's unembarrassable where you're concerned," Phil said. He took Stevie's hand and led her out to the trailer, where Teddy was waiting for them.

A.J., they discovered, had already untacked his horse, Crystal, and loaded her on the van. Stevie and Phil could give both horses hay and water when Teddy was loaded.

Phil removed Teddy's tack and handed it to Stevie. She stored it in the van's tack bin and then helped Phil brush the horse and put on his blanket.

Phil handed Stevie Teddy's lead rope. She took him to the rear of the van and walked him straight up the ramp. He didn't once hesitate or balk. He just followed her.

"You're incredible!" Phil declared.

"You just have to show the horse you know what you're doing," Stevie, said, coming down off the van. "I'll show you how."

"That's not all I meant," he told her, catching her by her hands.

"We've really got to go," Stevie said. "I mean it. This night isn't over yet."

"I mean it, too," Phil said. Then he leaned down and kissed her sweetly on the lips. Stevie was in a hurry, but she wasn't in such a hurry that she didn't have time for a kiss like that!

"Merry Christmas," he said.

"Happy Hanukkah," she said.

"Stevie! Is that you?" It was Lisa, calling out the door of the stable. "Come on!"

"We'll be right there," Stevie called back. She took Phil's hand. "Let's go. It's time."

"For what?" he asked.

"For Christmas," Stevie replied. "But just act natural, okay?"

Phil gave her a very strange look, but he followed her willingly.

"LORRAINE, REMEMBER THAT you've got to untack Patch before you give him water and food," Carole said. "It's removing the tack that will make him comfortable. Patch deserves that, doesn't he?"

"I'm sorry, Carole. I just always forget the order I'm supposed to do things. Maybe it's because I'm hungrier than I am uncomfortable."

Carole smiled. "Here, I'll give you a hand. I think your parents are outside and I bet there's a good Christmas Eve dinner waiting for you at home."

"Thanks," Lorraine said gratefully, accepting Carole's help.

When Carole was sure Lorraine could finish the job herself, she took Patch's tack to the tack room. She thought about Pretty Boy. As soon as she'd gotten inside and dismounted, she'd cross-tied him in the hallway and loosened his girth, but she'd been so busy helping the less-experienced riders that she hadn't had a minute to attend to him other than that. He deserved better treatment.

"Carole, I can't get this buckle!" Meg Durham complained, asking Carole for help. Pretty Boy would have to wait. Meg did need assistance. One of the things that Carole loved about Pine Hollow was that all the riders learned to take care of the horses they rode, and the way they learned was by getting help from other riders. Most of the time, it was wonderful. Tonight, though, Carole wished she could just look after her own horse.

"Here's a fresh bale." Red O'Malley, Pine Hollow's chief stablehand, appeared, dropping fifty pounds of hay on the floor outside the stall where she and Meg were working. That was something else she had to do. Carole took the tack from Meg, stowed it in the tack room, and returned to break the bale into flakes. At this rate, she'd never talk to Max to find out where she could stable Pretty Boy for the night.

"You need a hand?" Lisa asked.

"I sure do," Carole said. "All of a sudden, it seems like

nobody here knows how to do anything by themselves. Or else there's some kind of conspiracy going on to make me the last person finished here tonight."

"Oh, I don't think so," Lisa said. "Well, maybe not the *last*, exactly . . ." Carole knew her friend was teasing, but she wasn't really in the mood for it. Her day with Judy was over, the Starlight Ride was finished. Now, Christmas, the day she hadn't been looking forward to, was looming in front of her.

"Can I give you a hand, Carole?" Stevie asked, now approaching from the other side with Phil and A.J. in tow.

"Yes!" Carole said. "Could you go ask Max where he wants me to stable Pretty Boy for the night? Mr. Michaels will come over tomorrow or the next day to pick him up. Find out where we can keep him until then, okay?"

Lisa was about to answer when Stevie interrupted. "Why don't you go do that yourself?" she asked.

Carole couldn't believe her ears. Her perfectly healthy, unbusy friend stood around offering help, and the minute she asked for the teeniest favor, this same friend, one of her two best friends in the world, flat-out refused!

"Thanks a heap, Stevie," Carole said, now extremely annoyed. "Is it too much to ask you to break this bale into flakes for me while I track Max down?"

"I can probably manage," Stevie said calmly.

Carole stormed off. She'd about had it. If everybody in the world needed help from her, they could just go without it for a while. She had something she had to do for the horse she'd been riding. What did she need with their trouble and their silliness and forgetfulness? So what if Lorraine was hungry? What about Carole? So what if Meg couldn't handle the buckle on her horse's saddle? What about Pretty Boy's saddle? She was tired of being the stable slave! And when her own friend treated her like that, well—

"Hi, Carole," her father said.

"Dad! What are you doing here?" she asked. "I thought I was meeting you at the Lakes'—although the way Stevie's acting, I'm just as glad we don't have to go there."

"I think the way they say it in the movies is, 'I just happened to be in the neighborhood, so I thought I'd stop by.'"

"I'm glad," Carole said, and hugged him. He hugged her back. It was hard to be angry at anybody when her father was there.

"Did you have a good time on the Starlight Ride?" Colonel Hanson asked.

"Oh, yes! It was great. And I have so much to tell you about everything—about my day with Judy, about the ride, about all these funny pranks my friends were pulling, about this horse I got to use—oh, the horse." Suddenly, Carole remembered that she had something more important to do than to chat with her father. "Can you wait a few minutes? Then I'll tell you all about it."

"Sure I can wait, hon," Colonel Hanson said. "I've got all the time in the world just to hear about your day and this horse."

"Have you seen Max?"

"I'm right here, Carole. What's up?" Max asked, stepping out of Mrs. Reg's office.

"Where can I put Pretty Boy for the night?"

"Why don't you put him in his own stall?" Max said.

"No, I mean Pretty Boy, the horse I borrowed from Mr. Michaels. He'll come for him tomorrow or the next day."

Max shook his head. "I don't think Mr. Michaels will come for him at all," he said. "So put him in his own stall."

"What?" Carole said, and then she understood. She remembered that Mr. Michaels was selling Pretty Boy. He must have been sold to somebody who would keep him at Pine Hollow. That meant that maybe, just maybe, the new owner would let Carole ride him sometime.

"He's being boarded here?" she asked.

"Yep," Max said. "His new stall is the third one down this hallway. Show him to his room."

"I'll be right back," Carole told her father.

She got Pretty Boy from the other end of the hall, unclipped his lead, and took him to his new home.

There, standing by the doorway to Pretty Boy's stall, were Stevie, Lisa, Phil, A.J., her father, Max, Mrs. Reg, Red, Lorraine, Meg, and other riders.

"Are you all planning to study my untacking techniques?" Carole asked. She still felt a little annoyed that she was the only one working when there was so much to do.

Carole took Pretty Boy into his stall. It was sparkling clean and very welcoming.

"Hey, this place is all set up, isn't it?" Carole said, noticing the new buckets and fresh grooming gear. She looked at the sea of faces staring over the half door to the stall.

"What is going on here?" she said, now more confused than annoyed.

"Merry Christmas, my darling daughter," Colonel Hanson said.

"MINE? YOU MEAN Pretty Boy is mine, to own, to keep, to take care of, to ride? Mine?"

"That's what the papers say, Carole," Max said.

Carole didn't know who to hug first, so she started with her horse. He liked it a lot. He nuzzled her neck, and she hugged him some more as she cried with joy.

Next, still crying, she hugged her father.

"Oh, Daddy!" Carole said. "How could—I didn't—I mean—"

"You're not making any sense, girl, so stop talking," he said gently, returning her hug. "If you're wondering how I knew you wanted a horse, you're *really* not making any sense. All you have ever wanted was a horse. This is the time I decided you were old enough and grown-up enough to own one. If you're wondering how I found *this* horse for you, well, just ask your friends. They were in on it. They'll tell you the story. And then, if you're wondering how you ended up riding this horse tonight, well, I have no idea. I think it's some kind of miraculous coincidence."

"It was a coincidence, all right," Max said. "But I don't know about the miracle part. Both Judy and Mr. Michaels knew your father had bought Pretty Boy for you, so when you needed a way to get here, well, you can see what their thinking was."

Carole heard these words and understood them, but just barely. She had to ask, one more time.

"Is he really mine, Dad? Really?"

"Absolutely, one hundred percent. Your mother left me a little bit of money earmarked for you when she died. Actually, it was money she'd inherited from her own mother that she felt you should have. That's enough to pay for your horse, to take care of him, and to board him here for a few years. In a very real sense, Carole, this is a Christmas gift to you from both Mom and me."

The whole thing was like a dream come true. She was happier than she could ever remember being in her whole life. She got ahold of herself and stopped crying. There was something she needed to ask Max.

"About his name," she said. "Would it be okay if I change it? I mean, is it registered anyplace or anything? Does it matter what I call him?"

"His full legal name is Pretty Boy Floyd, and that's

what's on his registration papers. That's hard to change. However, you can *call* him anything you want. Horses are often called names other than their registered names and, in fact, it's not unusual for a new owner of a horse to pick a new name. Do you have something special in mind?"

"Well, not really," Carole said. "It's just that Pretty Boy seems so silly, kind of vain. It doesn't fit him. I'd like to have a name that's more like him—"

"Floyd?" A.J. suggested.

"Give me a break," Stevie said.

Then, for a few minutes, everybody had a suggestion. But nothing seemed quite right. Carole stood back in his stall and looked at her horse. His coat was a deep, rich brown and his black mane and tail were the velvety color of the night sky they had seen only a few minutes before on the Starlight Ride. The colors were beautiful, but they weren't all that distinctive. What was distinctive was his marking. There, on his forehead, was the lopsided six-pointed star. Carole had her answer.

"Ladies and gentlemen, I would like you to meet my new horse, Starlight."

"Perfect!" Stevie announced.

"Just right!" Lisa agreed.

"Welcome to our family," her father said.

"Maybe that *is* better than Floyd," A.J. joked.

Carole had a lot of work to do to see that Starlight was properly groomed and bedded down for the night. It was cold out and he'd had an active evening, to say the least!

She found that she loved doing everything for him just as much as she had known she would, maybe more. Starlight seemed to love it, too.

When she was finished and her friends had completed their chores, it was time to go home. Carole hugged Stevie and Lisa and wished them Merry Christmases. She hugged Phil and A.J. and whispered thanks to them for making Garnet "sick." She hugged Max and Mrs. Reg and thanked them for everything. But most of all, she hugged her father.

On the way home, she told him about her day and all the wonderful things that had happened. "This is the most incredible Christmas of my whole life," she said.

Her father squeezed her hand. "That's all I wanted, honey. You've made me happy just by being happy yourself. I don't want to get corny or anything, but you can't imagine the joy I felt, knowing that your mother and I had a hand in this Christmas for you. I don't want anything else for Christmas at all."

Carole sat up in her seat in the car. "You're not going to get off *that* easy," she said. "You've got a present or two coming from me, too, you know."

"I do?" he said. "I didn't see anything under the tree for me."

"Well, your presents aren't under the tree," she told him.

"Then where are they? I've looked over every single inch of the house and I couldn't find a thing!"

Carole laughed. "If I've actually found a hiding place out of your snoopy reach, I have no intention of telling you where it is. After all, I may—repeat *may*—want to give you something next year, too!"

"Drat! Foiled again!" he teased.

Carole realized then, sitting next to her father, that she had never really had any reason to worry about Christmas. She was filled with joy because of Starlight, but she'd have had a wonderful Christmas with her father no matter what. They missed her mother, but they did have each other, and that was very special and very precious to both of them. In a way, Carole thought, that was her very best Christmas present of all.

13

"How did your father like his socks?" Lisa asked Carole. The three girls were standing outside of Starlight's stall, having a Saddle Club meeting on the day after Christmas.

"He just loved them," Carole said. "He put them on right away and didn't take them off all day. He also liked the book and the record I gave him. The book was a history of rock from the fifties and the record went with it. He'll be hogging the stereo all the time now. I don't know if I'll ever get to hear any *real* music after this."

Carole wasn't really complaining. She didn't mind her father's music and, besides, she had a horse of her own so it seemed impossible that there could be anything to complain about ever again! "But enough about that. Here are your presents from me," Carole said, handing each of her friends two boxes. "Merry belated Christmas!"

Stevie opened the small box first. It was a pair of kid riding gloves. "You remembered!" she said, slipping them onto her hands.

"Of course I did. I ruined your last pair rescuing Samson out of the briar patch. I had to replace them in case I ever needed to borrow them again!"

Lisa opened the small box Carole had given her. Her present was also a pair of riding gloves, but these were string gloves, meant for warm weather. "They're beautiful!" Lisa said. "I guess you knew, didn't you?"

Carole nodded. "So did Stevie," she said. Mrs. Atwood had told both of them that Lisa's Christmas present was a one-week trip with her parents to a Caribbean island where, among other things, there was horseback riding. The Atwoods would be leaving in two days. Carole had wanted to help outfit Lisa for the trip.

"Open this one!" Stevie handed Lisa a very large box. Inside, Lisa found a pair of waterproof riding boots. "They were mine," Stevie told her. "I outgrew them and they're just your size now. You'll need them for riding in the ocean."

"Can you believe it?" Lisa asked dreamily. "Riding on the beach, with the sun, sand, water, and palm trees? I can't wait!"

"Sounds wonderful to me," Carole agreed. "To be honest, though, I'd rather stay here, with Starlight."

"I don't blame you," Stevie said. They all looked up at the horse, who was peering up over the door to his stall as if he were hanging on every word the girls were saying.

"Speaking of Starlight, that reminds me," Carole said. "What's the story about you two helping Dad get him for me?"

"Oh, that was fun!" Stevie laughed. "See, we ran into your dad the day we were at the mall, and he told us he wanted to get you a horse and asked if we had any ideas how he should go about it. So, I started to tell him he had to talk to Max, when Lisa said—"

"When I said I knew the perfect horse for you," Lisa interrupted. "Remember when my parents got the bright idea of buying me a horse?" she asked. "Around the same time Max was starting Horse Wise?" Carole and Stevie nodded. They remembered because Lisa had been so reluctant to tell them about it, thinking they'd be jealous. "Well, one of the horses I saw was Pretty Boy. I knew he was terrific the minute I saw him, but as soon as I was on him, I also knew he wasn't the horse for me. He needs a better rider than I am and he probably still needs some more training. I couldn't own him, but even then I knew you'd be perfect for him. So when your dad said he wanted to look for a horse for you, I told him he didn't have to. I already knew about one you'd love. Was I right?"

"You were right!" Carole said.

"Hi, girls. Have a good Christmas?" Judy Barker

greeted them. "Well, I know *you* did, Carole!" she teased, looking at Starlight. "How about your friends?"

"It was great," they both told her.

"You here to check on Starlight?" Carole asked.

Judy stepped into Starlight's stall and checked him over quickly. "Yes, and I'm glad to see he's fine," she said, approving his new quarters. "And I thought I ought to look at Garnet, too. Any problem there that I should know about?" she asked.

Carole tried to keep a straight face. She didn't really want to tell Judy what had happened, but before she could control it, her laughter erupted, and so did her friends'. They just couldn't help themselves. Almost without meaning to, they told Judy the entire story—including Veronica's pranks and the stall switching.

Judy, who was normally quite reserved and who definitely took horse health very seriously, was soon laughing along with them, especially when they got to the shaving cream. That explained Veronica's hysteria as well as Garnet's speedy and total recovery.

"Don't worry, I hosed her down and got all the soap off. She smells like a freshly shaved man," Stevie promised.

"Well, I can see everything is under control here," Judy commented. "I'm on my way back to Mr. Michaels's to see the newborn filly."

"So everything worked out all right there?" Carole

asked. She'd meant to call Judy and ask, but she'd been pretty busy herself.

"Just fine," Judy replied. "Within half an hour after you left, Carol was up and nursing."

"Carol? Huh?"

"Oh, didn't you know?" Judy said. "Mr. Michaels named the horse Carol—no e—for Christmas Carol. Isn't that sweet?"

"Well, sure," Carole-with-an-e said. "I like the idea that my horse has a sister with the same name as me!"

On that note, Judy left to continue her rounds. Carole planned to go out with her again the next day. This day, however, was saved for her friends—Stevie, Lisa, and Starlight.

"Back to presents," Stevie commanded. She'd been holding the other box from Carole for too long. It just had to be opened!

"Okay, so go ahead and open it," Carole said.

Stevie did. She unwrapped a pink sweat shirt with a horse screen-painted on it. The horse was a bay who looked a lot like Topside. "It's perfect!" Stevie told Carole.

"Now it's your turn," Carole said to Lisa.

"Is it the same?" Lisa asked, eyeing the box, which was the same shape as Stevie's had been.

"Not quite," Carole said. Lisa opened the box. Her sweat shirt was almost the same as Stevie's, except that her horse was a dappled gray who looked a lot like Pepper. "Wow!" she said. She and Stevie put on their new sweat shirts right away.

"You both look great," Carole said. "One thing I always say is that you can never have too many horsey clothes!"

Both Lisa and Stevie hugged and thanked her.

"Too bad you can't wear what we gave you," Lisa remarked.

"I *love* what you gave me," Carole insisted. Her friends' gift to her was a complete horse-care kit for Starlight. They'd gotten some things, like Starlight's blanket and halter secondhand, and lovingly cleaned them until they were spotless. Other things, like Starlight's buckets and his grooming gear, were brand-new, and they'd had Carole's name engraved on them for her. Best of all, Stevie and Lisa had bought a brass plaque for the door of his stall—the plaque that told everyone that Starlight was a privately owned horse. So far, the plaque only read

Carole Hanson

but soon, perhaps as soon as tomorrow, Max would take it to the shop where they'd put

STARLIGHT

above her name.

Carole took out her new currycomb and began to work on Starlight's coat. She wanted it to gleam all of the time.

"You know, the thing I don't get, Lisa," she remarked as she worked vigorously, "is how Stevie managed to keep not one, but two secrets—your trip and my horse."

"I don't know how she did it, either," Lisa said. "Her average secret-keeping time is much less than two weeks. It's more like two minutes!"

"Maybe it's because she's been distracted," Carole suggested. "She still hasn't been able to make up her mind about what she's going to wear to the big New Year's Eve dance with Phil Marston."

Stevie made a face. She didn't mind their teasing, but she didn't like to admit, even to her best friends, how much the dance had been on her mind. "Well, at least it gives me something to look forward to," Stevie said, defending herself.

"Speaking of Phil, I think it's time we made it official," Carole said. "He and A.J. both earned their way into The Saddle Club on Christmas Eve with the Garnet prank, don't you think?"

Stevie nodded, pleased. She'd wanted to invite Phil to join them ever since summer, but she was hoping her friends would suggest it. "I'll call him tonight and ask," she said.

"And you know what?" Lisa said. "The tie tack you gave him for Hanukkah will make a perfect Saddle Club pin for the boys."

Stevie's grin told her friends that she'd already thought of that.

"Can we get one for A.J.?" Carole asked.

"No problem," Stevie said. "I'll go back to the place I bought Phil's and buy another one. I'll give it to him from all of us when I see him at the New Year's Eve dance."

"Then it's decided. We're officially expanded," Carole said proudly.

"Growing bigger every day," Lisa said.

"And better, too," Stevie added.

"Oh, I don't know," Carole said. She hugged her horse and her friends at the same time. "It's hard to think that it could get any better than this!"

ABOUT THE AUTHOR

BONNIE BRYANT is the author of more than thirty books for young readers, including the best-selling novelizations of *The Karate Kid* movies and *Teenage Mutant Ninja Turtles* movie. The Saddle Club books are her first for Bantam Skylark. She wrote her first book eight years ago and has been busy at her word processor ever since. (For her first three years as an author, Ms. Bryant was also working in the office of a publishing company. In 1986, she left her job to write full-time.)

Whenever she can, Ms. Bryant goes horseback riding in her hometown, New York City. She's had many riding experiences in the city's Central Park that have found their way into her Saddle Club books—and lots which haven't!

The author has two sons, and they all live together in an apartment in Greenwich Village that is just too small for a horse.

Some things are for grown ups.
Some things are for kids.
But the best things are

Just For Girls

Petite Naté

Like *The Saddle Club*™ and *Starlight Christmas*,
Petite Naté™ is created especially for you.

A fragrant cologne to splash or spray-on, bubbles
and shampoo to turn your bath into an adventure, plus
talc and lotion for after-bath fun—it's all **Petite Naté.**
And it's all Just For Girls.

Happy Holidays to all our friends!

Love,
The Saddle Club
Carole. Lisa and Stevie

Offer available in U.S.

Jean Naté® Petite Naté™ © 1990 Revlon, Inc., Dist., N.Y., NY 10022

From Bantam-Skylark Books
IT'S

From Betsy Haynes, the bestselling author of the Taffy Sinclair books, comes THE FABULOUS FIVE. Follow the adventures of Jana Morgan and the rest of THE FABULOUS FIVE in Wakeman Jr. High.